"I won't leave you here to die!" Lyons shouted

"I'd do the same for you, specialist," Nate shot back. "I can't go anywhere with this leg wound, so I'm staying here. When their helicopter comes down in that clearing, I'll hit them. Give you time."

Lyons shook his head. "I'll tie you onto my back. I can carry you out."

Nate laughed. Then his hand whipped up and grabbed Lyons's shirt. He jerked the Able Team vet down until their faces were inches apart. "I can't make it out. I am dead. You will do what I say. You will get my wife and baby boy out or I will come back from hell and scream in your head until you die shaking."

Mack Bolan's

ABLE TEAM

ABLE TEAM
Ironman

Dick Stivers

A GOLD EAGLE BOOK FROM

W🌐RLDWIDE

TORONTO • NEW YORK • LONDON • PARIS
AMSTERDAM • STOCKHOLM • HAMBURG
ATHENS • MILAN • TOKYO • SYDNEY

First edition August 1985

ISBN 0-373-61219-2

Special thanks and acknowledgment to G. H. Frost
for his contributions to this work.

Printed in Canada

1

Lyons saw only police and customs officers.

No soldiers, he thought. Can't be Guatemala.

But the immigration clerk had stamped his passport with the quetzal in flight of Guatemala. The wad of money in his pocket featured the faces of generals—the Quicherno hero Tecun Uman and Creole heroes Orellana, Barrios, Granados.

Lyons paused in the center of the arriving and customs area and scanned the second floor. At the railing above, Guatemalans watched for their friends and relatives. Behind them, Lyons saw the sign of the Bank of Guatemala and signs advertising a messenger service, books and liquor. But no soldiers.

A coup? Possibly. A coup would explain the absence of soldiers. The generals would need their men to besiege the national palace. Or to close down the garrisons of their opposition.

Peace? Lyons laughed. Not in Guatemala! If the army ran out of guerrillas to fight, the generals would use the peace as a chance to plot a coup.

Behind him, he heard German and Italian. Tourists crowded around a Banco de Guatemala Caja de Cambio. They signed American Express travelers checks and pushed the checks through the window to the clerk.

One for one. One dollar buys one quetzal. In Miami, a dollar bought one quetzal thirty-eight centavos. In Washington D.C., Lyons had checked his sources and learned that on the Guatemalan street market, one dollar bought one quetzal and forty eight centavos. But in Washington, through his sources, Lyons had bought quetzals at two percent above the international-bank purchase rate: every one of his dollars bought one quetzal seventy-five centavos.

The tourists lost almost half their money by changing their travelers' checks at the official rate.

Lyons saw his blue backpack lurching along the luggage conveyor. He rushed over and grabbed it, grunting with the weight. Like the pack he used on missions, the pack had an internal frame and padded shoulder and hip straps. This pack differed only in the color. Knowing that his night-black pack might not pass Guatemalan security regulations, he had brought a navy-blue pack.

His clothes and personal kit took only a fraction of the oversized pack's interior. Instead of ammunition, grenades, envelopes of freeze-dried rations and first-aid equipment, he had filled the 5275-cubic-inch interior with gifts for Nate and his family.

A customs inspector with Mayan features but the amber eyes of a Creole motioned for Lyons to set the pack on a conveyor. Lyons dropped it on the black rubber belt and unzipped the back panel to expose the interior. Lyons had packed all his clothes and gifts in one-gallon Ziploc bags. The inspector glanced at Lyon's phony passport, then at his face, comparing the photo of the bearded blond man with the man in front of him. Nodding, the inspector handed back the passport and turned to the pack. He smiled at Lyons's packing.

"*Bueno*...very good, Señor Stone."

The customs man made conversation that Lyons could not follow with his limited understanding of Spanish. He watched as the inspector squeezed a few bags, then plunged his hands deep into the bundles of clear plastic to feel around in the corners.

Lyons knew that the inspector searched for weapons. Had the military precision of the packing made the inspector suspicious? Did he wonder why the *norteamericano*, Mr. Stone, who looked like a soldier, wore a beard? If he found the double-edged boot knife, would it qualify as a military weapon?

For a moment Lyons doubted the smarts of taking a vacation in a country where he had worked. He remembered the reaction of his partners when he told them he wanted to take off for a week and backpack in Guatemala.

Gadgets laughed and shook his head with disbelief. "We've worked there, Ironman! We've killed people down there. And you want to go along? You and a Spanish-English dictionary and your fucked-up attitude?"

Blancanales had suggested an alternative. "You wouldn't need to speak Spanish in Hawaii."

"But I want to go to Guatemala. Go see how Nate's doing with the hundred grand we paid him."

"Then go to Hawaii!" Gadgets jived. "That Nate dude probably took the money and got gone from the crazy nation of Nazis. Probably bought a condo at Waikiki.''

"He wrote me a letter. Said everything was okay.''

"Okay for a righteous payback!" Gadgets had spoken seriously, not joking. "How do you know it's Nate that wrote to you? How do you know it's not a trap?''

"Because Nate wouldn't set me up like that.''

"Go, man. Go. But don't forget to say your prayers. Lo, though I walk through the nation of death, I shall fear no evil—''

Lyons added the next line, "For I am the —''

"The rudest!" Gadgets jived.

"The meanest—" Lyons continued.

"Perhaps the most dangerous,'' Blancanales added with a smile.

"And most definitely five kinds of scary, scary dude,'' Gadgets interjected.

"That ever walked,'' Lyons concluded.

"Amen,'' Gadgets added. "Lotsa luck, Lyons. But while you're gone, we're running an ad for replacements, just in case. All right?''

Now Lyons wondered if Gadgets had been joking or serious. In his peripheral vision he saw two customs inspectors coming up behind him. He forced himself to relax. He could do nothing. If they grabbed him, if they hauled him into a detention room, if they dragged him across the airport to the headquarters of the elite Panther Battalion, he could do nothing more than protest the treatment and demand to call the U.S. Embassy.

Act like a tourist…because that's all you are this time, he thought.

The other inspectors reached into his pack. One pulled out a bag of rhythm-and-blues and jazz cassettes. The other found two pairs of children's running shoes. But they didn't examine the contents. They talked to one another; Lyons understood only that they liked the Ziploc bags. Finally they replaced the bags in the pack. The first inspector pressed a rubber stamp on some of the bags, marking the plastic with a blue-ink customs seal, then motioned Lyons past. As Lyons leaned down to zip up the backpack, the inspector had already gone to the next arriving passenger.

Keep your paranoia under control, Lyons told himself. No one knows who you are. And even if they did, they might not care. You were here two governments ago. The bad guys are long gone. Some of them you killed. The others are in Chile or El Salvador or Miami. In fact Guatemala might be the safest place around. They'd never expect you to risk coming here alone....

As he stepped out of the terminal, ten different taxi drivers competed for his attention. He ignored the porters who offered to carry his pack. Then he saw the soldiers.

In camouflage fatigues and black berets, they lounged at the side of the taxi-parking area, their Galil assault rifles resting across their legs. They talked with one another, drinking sodas, ignoring the taxi drivers and tourists. Lyons noted that all the Galils had their fire-selector levers down to full-auto.

Standard for Guatemala. The at-ease soldiers reassured Lyons. No coup today. No serious action. Maybe an accidental discharge, but no ambush for a *norteamericano* specialist on a search-and-relax mission.

One taxi driver polished his car, a late-model Dodge. Lyons glanced inside and saw spotless upholstery, carefully sewn where riders' luggage had torn the vinyl. He opened the back door for himself and slid inside. The driver folded his polishing cloth and closed the door for his passenger.

"*Buenas tardes, señor.* Where are you going?"

"*Huehuetenango,*" Lyons answered.

The driver looked at him. He did not comment until he sat down behind the steering wheel and started the engine. He finally said, "*Dos cientos cincuenta quetzales.* Two hundred fifty dollars."

Lyons corrected himself. "*Quiero un camioneta a Huehuetenango. Donde hay la parada?*"

"Oh," the driver said, laughing. "You want a *bus* to Huehue! That is different! I take you to Ruta Limas...only eight quetzales. Okay?"

"*Sí.*"

As the taxi accelerated to ground level, brilliant midday glare made Lyons squint. He put on his sunglasses and watched the lawns and tropical flowers of the landscaping flash past. After a few hundred yards the long curving lane merged with a boulevard. The driver whipped the taxi through three lanes of trucks, buses and cars.

So different. Same city, same streets. But last time, on the trail of murderers and international weapons smugglers, they had walked into a setup. Their liaison men had intended to drive them around in the city, in circles, while a kill team assembled to execute him and his partners. Thanks to the electronic wizardry of

Gadgets, Able Team had turned the setup around. They had walked into it knowing every move of the Fascists. Then Able Team hit them and broke out. Three men in a foreign city, hunted by the Fascist International and Guatemalan traitors....

Almost two years ago. They had taken a plane on fifteen minutes' notice. The call for Lyons had woken him and Flor in a Washington, D.C., hotel room.

Flor....

Lyons had been a different man then. Mission first. No doubts. No hesitation. Flor would be there when he got back, and Lyons would get back. Lyons the immortal.

It was Flor Trujillo who didn't come back.

Nothing could bring her back to life. And the time he had with her lived in the shadow of the time he could have taken, but didn't. Now he had only memories. And nightmares of an exploding helicopter and the charred flesh and bones that remained of Flor....

The last time he'd been in Guatemala he'd walked into the midst of the Fascist International with the perfume and sweat of Flor Trujillo still on his body.

It was so different this time. No one was trying to kill him. No partners. No weapons. Alone.

Lyons looked up. The taxi had passed through two zones—the divisions of the sprawling city that had confused him and his partners the two years before. He saw the modern office buildings of the national administration center, the Banco de Guatemala and the offices of the Social Security Institute.

A banner hung across the institute's facade declaring a *Huelga de los Trabadores*. Lyons could not understand all the declaration. But he saw the workers passing out leaflets at the entrances.

Things had changed. Workers on strike? Passing out leaflets only a mile from the national-police headquarters? A few years before, the workers at the local Coca-Cola franchise had gone on strike. Perhaps the workers had thought transnational corporations honored the Bill of Rights. The American manager knew how to break the strike; he denounced the strikers. *'Desconocidos'* immediately murdered twelve labor leaders. In the Guatemala Lyons knew, workers feared the word "strike" like death. Guatemala had a tradition of settling strikes by having the strikers "disappear."

But now the country had a new government, and things had apparently changed.

Nothing had changed on the streets. Motorized chaos ruled the avenues. Motorcycles wove through the bumper-to-bumper lanes of cars and trucks and troop carriers, buses braked to take or unload passengers, then accelerated away in clouds of diesel smoke. Only the one-way traffic flow maintained movement. Lyons realized that some anonymous urban planner had extended the life of the capital by twenty years by limiting the north-south *avenidas* and east-west *calles* to alternating lanes of one way. If that unknown planner had not done so, Guatemala City would have become like Colombo in Sri Lanka, like the cities of Asia, like New York City during the Christmas season—disasters every minute of the day.

Then Lyons's senses snapped with alarm.

The taxi driver had passed the Terminal de Autobuses Extraurbanos minutes ago. While Lyons had daydreamed about Flor and considered the changes in Guatemalan labor relations and studied the traffic patterns, the taxi driver continued on to…where?

Leaning forward, Lyons glanced into the front seat. The driver had both hands in sight. Lyons saw no newspaper or magazine that might conceal a pistol. Making a pretense of leaning out the opposite window, Lyons scanned the fronts of the shops and apartments, then glanced down into the space between the front seat and the driver's door. No pistol. Finally Lyons spoke to the driver:

"This isn't the way to Extraurbanos. Where are we going?"

"Rutas Limas, *señor*. It is better—good buses for Huehue. The best! Look!"

Two blocks ahead a gleaming Mercedes tour bus with high panorama windows turned into traffic and accelerated away without the usual gray pall of diesel pouring from its exhaust pipe.

"You see? A tourist bus. I take you there."

Paranoia again. Lyons relaxed as the driver sped through three turns and braked in front of a gray concrete building. Deep inside, mechanics worked on the suspension of another Mercedes bus. The driver called out to a worker pushing a freight cart. Lyons couldn't follow the rapid Spanish question and answer exchange. The driver shrugged and turned.

"I'm sorry, my friend. No more buses. We go to Extraurbanos."

2

Valium solved the paranoia. Lyons downed five milligrams and took a gulp of lukewarm orange pop. Then he waited for the bus to leave, his legs stretched out, his nylon jacket secured to the handrail of the seat in front of him.

A government psychiatrist had prescribed Valium and Librium for his nightmares. Ten milligrams of Valium to put him to sleep, five milligrams of Librium to keep him asleep. Lyons added three shot glasses of eighty-proof vodka to the dosage. That gave him six hours of dreamless unconsciousness. He only used the pills when he had been inactive during the day. Physical exhaustion always proved to be a better sedative. But sometimes meetings and briefings kept him in a chair all day and into the evening. Those nights often proved to be the worst: after hours of terse, brutal language describing the torture of American operatives or the mass murders of foreigners suspected of cooperation with U.S. agencies, after daylong slide shows of satellite photos, corpses, identikit composites, corpses, weapons, corpses, "disappeared" families, corpses, his imagination exploded with horror. He maintained the mask of the stone-cold operative for the meetings, but alone—without the neutral decor of the offices, the sardonic jokes of his partners, the never-ending onrush of information—he could not keep his mind blank.

It all came back in his sleep, his unconscious vomiting the horror and suffering and cruelty into the more-than-real world of his dreams. Sometimes he escaped a nightmare by going out into the early-morning isolation and running for hours, until exhaustion guaranteed dreamless sleep. But when meetings kept him in the cities of the east coast, he could not use the sedative of exercise: the frigid weather, the crime and the always-possible threat of Soviet, Libyan, Fascist—whoever—counteraction trapped him in the hotels. Long-distance runs in Washington, D.C., would only give the chaos of crime or the assassins of some foreign—or American—gang an opportunity to snuff him or kidnap him for interrogation. New York, with its population of United Nations "diplomats," offered variations on the threats.

Sedatives and a bottle of vodka from room service—all paid for by the federal government—became the expedient key to dreamless sleep. And now, five milligrams of Valium and an Agua de Naranja turned off the paranoia and turned on a wide and uncharacteristic smile. Other passengers took their seats, talking to one another in Guatemalan Spanish and indigenous languages. Some wore the polyester and nylon of the twentieth century, others the hand-woven *traje* of their mountain pueblos. They glanced at Lyons as they passed, then continued to their seats.

Good, Lyons thought. No one looked twice. I'm no one special.

At the front of the bus two hippies took seats. One wore his curly blond hair in a tangled ponytail that hung down his back. His girlfriend had not bothered to even tie back her rat nest of hair. Both wore what they believed to be *traje*, the woman a dirty *huipile* and a dark skirt, the man cotton peon pants of stained and filthy white cotton. But for a shirt, he wore an embroidered and brocaded *huipile* cut down the front to create a vest.

The male hippie, dressed in a *huipile* took the attention of the Guatemalans in the same way that the sight of a filthy ragged transvestite would take the attention of commuters on a bus in the United States—everyone went quiet and stared.

Yet, unlike the United States, no one responded to the hippie with ridicule or violence.

The Guatemalans smiled to one another but said nothing aloud. One Guatemalan—a Quichenero in the brilliant red-gold-white pants and red-yellow shirt of Santa Cruz de Quiche region—saw Lyons staring at the foreigners. Lyons the *norteamericano* only smiled and shook his head. The Quichenero laughed quietly but said only, "Jippies."

The hippies talked loudly in French and Lyons watched the cargo carts pass in the street. The Valium diminished his loathing of the boy and girl travelers to a very mild and nonlethal awareness of their absurdity.

Looking away, he watched a cargo man in the street hauling a handcart loaded with perhaps a thousand pounds of cornmeal in sacks. The small man, weighing no more 110 pounds, strained at the pull handles and crossbars like a beast of burden. No, Lyons realized, not like an animal. Like a man trying to feed his family. No animal would work like that. Even with the lashing of whip, no animal would strain against the crossbar, every muscle and tendon of his legs standing out like sculpture from his skin.

Indígena women of Sacatequepez, Agua Calientes, Momostenango, lined the curbs. They sat on squares of plastic, their baskets of vegetables displayed in front of them. Despite the flies and filth of the street, all the Guatemalans looked clean. Even the sweat-soaked cart man wore a clean, though patched and repatched, polyester shirt.

Hippies undercut the standards of the Third World, Lyons thought. If they want to be counterculture, why don't they present a "counter" worth seeing, rather than a walking eyesore?

The driver revved the engine and the bus lurched, then slowly eased forward through the hundreds of shoppers, laborers and vendors. The driver tapped the air horn every few seconds, and finally the bus cleared the crowds and the driver accelerated. Lyons watched the hundreds of multi-colored shop fronts flash past and...

He woke to pines and cloud-swept mountains. Vicente Fernandez sang from the driver's cassette player, his cries of lost love deliberately forlorn and sentimental—the soft side of machismo. Next to Lyons, a woman in the *huipile* of Totonicapan fed her three children corn-husk-wrapped tamales from a plastic bag stamped with the Jordache logo. The children pushed wads of beans and corn dough into their mouths and watched the blond, bearded stranger next to them watch them.

The woman glanced to Lyons with proud, Mayan disdain and then ignored him utterly. But as she dropped the empty greasy cornhusks on the sheet metal of the bus floor, she carefully avoided Lyons's gray slacks and his cordura and leather hiking boots.

Lyons checked his watch. After five. Running out of time if he wanted to make Azatlan tonight. But the taxi driver and the bus *ayudante*—the driver's assistant—had told him that this bus went direct to Huehuetenango, *"Directo!"* He had to get off twenty minutes before Huehue, where the side road to Azatlan crossed the Pan-American Highway.

There he would take another bus for an hour or two. Then a final bus to Azatlan. Nate had written instructions. His letter stressed, with heavy underscoring, "start in the morning." But then Pam Am did not arrange the company's flight schedules to make bus travel in Guatemala convenient. If Lyons got there late, too bad. Better than waiting a night in the capital.

"Señor Rubio! Aquí está su carreterra." The *ayudante* pointed to the roadway.

Lyons knew that *rubio* meant fair-haired, and it only reinforced his belief that he was going to stand out like a sore thumb among the Hispanics.

A minute later Lyons stood in the cold wind, his pack in the dust beside him. The late-afternoon sun warmed one side of his body but the wind chilled the other side. His gray polyester slacks did not provide much protection. He put his hands inside his jacket and waited as cars and trucks sped past on the Pan-American Highway.

Dry cornfields and pine forests extended into the distance. Lyons stood on a ridge overlooking fields and mountains and villages. The road he would take cut across the hillsides, zigzagging up a mountain, then disappeared over the ridgeline. Behind him, he saw forested mountains rising against the sky. Clouds swept over the peaks and ridges, enclosing the valleys and clefts within the mountains in darkness, as if the wind-torn storm carried the night.

A horn startled him and he turned as a twenty-year-old pickup truck rattled to a stop. *Quicheneros* in the *traje* of two different villages leaped from the back. As the dust swept past Lyons, he grabbed his backpack by the luggage strap. The weight of shoes, magazines, cassettes and toys almost pulled him over sideways. He struggled upright and lurched over to the truck, calling out to a young man who looked like the *ayudante:*

"Azatlan?"

"Dos paradas más."

"Two more stops," Lyons muttered.

He recognized the name of the town past the Azatlan turnoff. He swung his pack over the side of the pickup.

Un quetzal, señor." As the *ayudante* pocketed the dollar, the driver threw the pickup into reverse. Lyons struggled to find a comfortable place in the back of the truck as the pickup rattled over the dirt road, the swaying and lurching throwing Lyons from side to side. A tire hit a hole and metal slammed into Lyons's tailbone. He immediately rearranged his pack to provide him a backrest. But he had nothing to pad his butt.

Unzipping his pack, he felt through his gear and found his bag of clothes. He jerked out the oversized packing bag and sat on it. Perfect.

He leaned back and watched the mountains and forests pass. A mile above him storm clouds surged over the ridge like waves crashing over a seawall. The chill wind of the changing weather whipped at him, but the afternoon sun on his face and black jacket warmed him.

The truck passed a group of women working in the fields. A boy worked with them, methodically hacking down dry, yellow cornstalks with machetes. Against the cold, the boy wore black wool coats, the women heavy shawls over their *huipiles*. Some of the shawls sagged with the round weight of babies. The women worked bent over at their waists, bundling the cornstalks and tying them together with lengths of twine.

As they looked up at the truck, Lyons saw the faces of the women set in grimaces, every face telling a story of a life of dawn-to-dusk work, childbirth and hardship. Dust paled their hair and clothing. Then the wind carried the pickup's dust over the women. Coughing, without wasting another moment to watch the truck and the blond, bearded stranger, the women resumed their work, stooping and gathering. Lyons lost sight of the women in the screen of dust.

For the next two hours he rode in the back of the truck as the afternoon became dusk. *Indígenas* boarded and left the truck like passengers on a bus line. Sometimes they tried to make conversation with the bearded *norteamericano*. But Lyons's Spanish did not allow conversation.

The truck stopped once for two woodcutters who lifted rope-tied bundles of firewood into the back. Lyons helped them wrestle their loads over the side.

Surprised, they thanked him in Spanish, then talked with one another in what Lyons thought might be *Quiche*.

A few minutes later the figures of a man and woman appeared in the semidarkness and got in the back. They said nothing to Lyons or the woodcutters. Wrapping their faces with shawls, the woman spoke quickly and sharply to her man, evidently berating him.

The truck lurched and the firewood shifted. A woodcutter braced the load to prevent the wood from falling on the woman, and the man and the woman spat out curses in their language. But the woodcutter spoke to them in Spanish. Then Lyons realized that the two woodcutters and the man and woman did not speak the same language. The two groups, living only a few valleys apart, needed Spanish as a common language.

When the woodcutters halted the truck, slapping on the side panels to signal the driver, Lyons helped them again. He steadied the loads while they slipped on their *mecapales*—straps worn across their foreheads—and then tilted the loads onto their backs. Their foreheads and backs bore the loads. They did not have shoulder straps.

Lyons saw the woodcutters turn, their faces red in the glow of the truck's taillights, and wave thanks to him, then darkness and dust took them. The man and woman sharing the truck with him remained silent, black shapes, not even speaking to one another.

A glow appeared behind the mountain range to the east, and minutes later, Lyons saw the moon rise—at first a white fragment, then a brilliant white arc above a jagged ridgeline, finally the full disc of the moon. To the north and west, the moon illuminated the banks of clouds. But above, Lyons saw the star-swirling dome of the night sky, free of pollution, lights or planes—infinite.

Lyons scanned the panorama—the rising full moon, the moonlit forests and mountains, the brilliant-blue fields, the valleys and ridges extending into the distance—and loved it.

For an instant, as the truck lurched and banged along the dirt road, he felt like singing and shouting, jumping up and putting his face to the wind, riding the truck like a surfboard, hanging ten on the cab, looking down through the windshield and promising the driver and *ayudante* a hundred quetzales each if they'd floor it, burn rubber in a crazed dirt-road wheelie, break the chains of gravity, launch the truck to fly over the forests and mountains, straight into that dome of infinite space so he could streak through the heavens....

The truck braked and a head appeared out the passenger window. *Su carreterra!"*

Moving fast, Lyons picked up his pack of clothes. He slapped it a few times to knock off the dust and dirt and wood chips, then unzipped his pack and shoved the bag deep inside. He pulled the backpack's zipper tight. Grunting, he got the pack balanced on the side rail. The two *indígenas* ignored him, as if the truck had stopped for a traffic signal. Lyons jumped down and shrugged into the shoulder straps. As he jammed the hip-strap buckle together, the truck started away. Lyons ran a few steps.

"I am going to Azatlun. Which direction?" Lyons shouted in Spanish.

By the dashboard light he saw a sawed-off shotgun across the legs of the *ayudante*. A hand pointed past Lyons.

"And when is there a bus?"

"There is none, no bus at night!"

Lyons stood in the swirling dust. No bus at night? That's why Nate told him to start in the morning!

He stood at an intersection in the mountains. Preceded by a fan of yellow light, the taillights of the truck swayed and bounced away, the sounds of the springs and of rocks banging in the wheel wells continuing even after the lights disappeared in the trees. In the moonlight he saw another dirt road angling up to the ridgeline.

Lyons became aware of the silence. After hours on the bus, with its voices and cassette music, then another two hours in the back of the pickup, springs squeaking, rocks clattering, he heard only wind.

Cold wind flowed through the pines. Cornstalks clattered and scraped against other cornstalks. Dry grass clicked. Even with his firefight-damaged hearing, he seemed to hear the vast envelope of the atmosphere as it rushed over the earth, making everything around him move.

"Boy Scout's motto..." he whispered to himself. If Gadgets had been there, they would have jived a duet of "Be prepared!" but Lyons let his voice fade as he took out his compass.

The tritium-headed arrow gave him his orientation. Then he pulled out his plastic-protected map and his penlight. With the brilliant moonlight, he almost didn't need the penlight.

By force of habit, he crouched against a tree to hide the faint light cupped in his hand. As he checked the map he wondered if he needed to conceal the penlight glow. So what if he didn't hide his light? Who would see it? And what if they did? In Nate's letters, he had told Lyons that peace had finally come to the area. But then again, the *ayudante* in the pickup truck had carried a sawed-off 12-gauge. No one carried that kind of firepower without a reason.

The map confirmed what he saw around him.

"Only one road...."

3

Wind and moonlight.

Despite the weight of his pack and the steep grade of the road, Lyons maintained an even pace up the mountain. The cold wind forced him to keep his hands inside his jacket. If he had to carry a weapon, his hands would have gone numb minutes after he left the truck. But he traveled this time as a tourist, not a "specialist."

He leaned into the gusts, feeling the wind chill his scalp and face and throat. Sometimes wind went down the neck of his T-shirt like a splash of cold water. The nylon of his jacket kept his torso warm, the walking kept his legs warm. His back, protected from the wind by his jacket and the pack, streamed with sweat.

Around him, the pines surged and swayed. Branches creaked as wood rubbed against wood. A rushing sound—creaking wood, bending branches, millions of pine needles thrown against millions of others—preceded every gust, giving Lyons a moment to brace himself before the wind struck.

He walked through stretches of bright moonlight and starlit darkness, his eyes adjusting easily to the light and shadows. Only when clouds passed overhead and he happened to be walking through shadows did the darkness become complete. After stumbling several times, instead of using his penlight, he simply paused when both clouds and shadows denied him vision.

In a moment of darkness he stopped in the middle of the dirt road and checked his watch. He had walked for two hours, but still had not reached the crest of the mountain. He did not bother to check his map. He knew he had not missed a turnoff or taken the wrong fork of a road.

Lyons carried a reduction-photocopy of a National Security Agency satellite-generated contour graph as a map. To avoid very serious problems with Guatemalan customs officers or an observant policeman, he had erased all the computer codes and trimmed off the top-secret markings before laminating it in plastic. The map showed every highway, road, dirt track—and some of the foot trails and houses—in the area.

There had been no other roads. Only this one dirt road leading to the other asphalt road.

As he stood in the darkness, the wind chilling his sweat, he pulled down breath after breath, drinking, gulping the cold, pure air. He smelled and tasted only trees. Then a gust of wind brought the bitter taste of dust.

The dust triggered a memory. Standing there in the darkness, high in the mountains of the altiplano, he remembered the dust of San Diego the day Flor Trujillo died. The dust blown by the rotor-storm of helicopters, the dust and cordite of the airport kills, the grit and sting of dust when he walked away crying from the scorched wreckage that had been her helicopter and the carrion, the bones and black ash that had been her body.

He stood in the darkness, his skin suddenly flashing with chills, and remembered her voice and her anger and her love, her touch—and he turned and wandered away on the road, as if movement in the present could leave behind him the past he remembered and would always remember.

Stumbling, he kicked rocks. He staggered a few steps before regaining his stride. Somewhere a dog barked. Moonlight returned and Lyons increased his stride, as if trying to leave his shadow and memories behind him. The dog continued barking, and Lyons figured the dog to be hundreds of yards downwind from him, across a small valley and somewhere on a ridge patterned by the rectangles of cornfields. Perhaps the dog had heard him, heard the rocks he kicked, his boots scuffing. Perhaps the dog smelled his sweat.

Marveling at the acute senses of the watchdog only occupied a few seconds of Lyons's thoughts. To avoid thinking of Flor he tried to calculate the distance remaining to where the dirt road met the all-weather road coming from the southwest. It was the same road that now-dead Luis had taken two years before.

Dead Flor. Dead Luis. Dead Konzaki. So many dead. He had met combat vets who talked about friends, raving about their adventures and brotherly trust, only to learn as the stories continued that the friends had died. When Lyons had asked about their other friends, what their living friends did now, after the war and exploits, wanting to learn if the vets continued being brothers after the danger ended, the vet with the stories had said, "All my friends are dead," and then laughed. Lyons had wondered what that laugh meant. Maybe now he knew.

The laugh, the joke, the story and the laughing that told the truth and masked the truth. "He was my friend, he was more than my brother because my brother never ran up against a tree line flashing with AK muzzles to drag my ass to cover and now he's dead because he took his turn on point and stepped on a mine instead of me." The truth and the laugh to mask the truth of the loss.

Flor didn't like Lyons taking over the airborne pursuit of two trucks carrying fugitives and weapons, so she had commandeered another helicopter and joined the pursuit. A gunman in the back of a pickup truck had one rocket-propelled grenade designed to punch holes through three hundred millimeters of steel-plate armor, one rocket loaded in the launcher. Then two helicopters appeared. Flor's pilot had not seen the rocket launcher and flew straight in for the attack.

Flor took the rocket.

Lyons lived. Flor died. Lyons watched her helicopter disintegrate and fall in a shower of flame.

Blancanales killed the man who killed Flor, but Flor did not live again. The three men of Able Team had killed every gunman and driver in the two trucks, but Flor did not live again.

Like Gadgets said, "Go crazy, Ironman. Kill all the bad guys, but the payback won't bring her back."

And the killing didn't.

Lyons did not even have the old-time stories to bring her back, just for a few minutes as a memory. Talking about her, thinking about her, ripped through his mind like a knife. He tried hard to force the thoughts from his mind as he stomped his boots on the rocks and rutted earth of the road.

Then, his eyes focused on scenes in his memory, scenes past and beyond changing, he went over the crest and he saw the valley of Azatlan spread out before him.

In a valley between vertical mountains, surrounded by rolling hills and patchwork fields, the lights of the village shimmered in the glowing atmosphere. The dark line of a small river cut the lights and pale moonlit fields.

At the end of the long, narrow valley, cliffs rose from the forests. Masses of clouds crowned the black cliffs. Blue with moonlight, the clouds walled the northern horizon.

Wind shrieked past Lyons, dying to a droning hum as a gust faded. And that drone brought another memory, a story of reincarnation for warriors told by a Chicano ex-low-rider devotee of Huitzilopochtli, the Nahua god of war, who gave all the brave men who died in his name the reward of eternal beauty, endless reincarnations as living creatures of beauty.

And Lyons looked at the beauty of the world and laughed, the rage and despair and lost love twisting his mind becoming a moment of all-knowing joy—there is no death, only life. Individuals come and go, but life continues, the world continues, the stars continue, the galaxies breathing in and breathing out, every breath a hundred billion years, the infinite continuing, death an impossibility because life-the-infinite continued.

Lyons had no reason to despair, because soon he would be dead, too, killed in combat or dead of old age. Only a flashing moment separated birth and death, and he would soon join Flor and all his other dead and soon-to-be dead friends and enemies in another spin of life.

Standing on the ridge, the wind on him like the hands of the woman he remembered, Lyons had his moment of understanding and joy.

Then he continued to the asphalt road and started down into the valley. The downhill grade made his legs cramp, but he ignored the pain and after a few minutes the cramps went away, and he had a good time because he discovered he could skip, even with the weight of his bundled gifts, down the road in the moonlight and wind.

Dogs ended his philosopher-fool act.

The first dog sprang out of a roadside ditch and dived at Lyons's ankle. His combat-honed reflexes took over in midskip, his boot flicking out, the toe impacting exactly at the tip of the dog's nose. There was a yelp and scratching of claws, then the dog blurred back to the safety of the ditch. Barking followed Lyons for a hundred yards.

All down the road, dogs barked. "What is this?" Lyons said out loud. "I was having a good time and now…"

Two dogs ran from a walled compound. Lyons snatched a rock from the roadside and drew back his arm to throw. The dogs stopped. They barked and crept. Then another dog appeared on the other side of the road.

Lyons walked backward, watching for other dogs, gathering more rocks. He walked fast—no skipping now—spinning every few steps to threaten the dogs that followed him.

Two years before, he had passed these same houses. No corn grew in the fields. No fires burned in the hearths. No clothes hung on lines. Bullet holes had pockmarked the whitewashed walls. Burned roofs had collapsed into the fire-gutted houses. The one dog he had seen then ran and hid when their car passed.

All the people of the area had fled, abandoning their homes, taking their families to safety.

Able Team, with the help of Nate and his Quiche-nero friends, had wiped out the mercenary army of Unomundo, ending the terror against the people of Azatlan. The people had returned to their homes and fields.

And now their dogs tried to eat the *norteamericano* who had fought for the pueblo.

Lyons aimed at an onrushing dog, leading it slightly, and threw. He heard the whistle of the rock through the air, and his eyes tracked the spinning missile he willed into his target, seeing it impact behind the dog's head, where the neck met the shoulders. He heard the heavy thump of rock on flesh and the simultaneous yelp of pain and surprise. The dog veered away, and two other mutts followed it into the safety of the brush.

Claws scratched on asphalt and Lyons sidestepped, kicking a dog as its wide jaws, the jagged teeth blue in the moonlight, went past him. His boot sank into soft flesh, the kick lifting the dog off the road and throwing it, doubled over, into the ditch. The dog panted and tried to howl.

That example kept all the others back. Walking fast, Lyons left the pack behind. The barking finally faded, but he still held the rocks. There would be more houses along the road, and more dogs.

Strange how immediate problems eclipsed his memories, he thought. His moment of transcendence over all the bad memories and fears had been brought crashing down by a bunch of barking dogs. What about gurus? If they made the astral plane, floating above all the suffering and pain, did that make them exempt from worldly shit like dogs asserting their territorial rights?

In the quiet, with only the wind breaking the complete silence, he heard a rock clicking on the asphalt. A pebble had gotten jammed into the sole of his boot.

Dogs heard the faint clicking and barking once again broke the night. A hundred yards away, Lyons saw a dark house. A pale dog ran through the garden and stood waiting for him in the center of the road, barking.

Lyons shouted a warning, not words but a single guttural sound, bestial and threatening. At the same time, he visualized the image of his teeth closing on a miniature dog, the dog writhing, blood spurting....

The dog in front of him was suddenly quiet. It scurried into the darkness. Had the bestial shout done the trick? Or the telepathic assault?

Rocks proved to be more dependable than noise or psychic violence. In the next hour, as Lyons left the mountain and hiked across the flat valley floor, he scored two hits on aggressive dogs.

The dogs and beauty of the night kept his mind occupied. However, as he approached the village, he realized that he had not seen another person. Nor had a car or a truck passed him on the road, in either direction.

In the night, Azatlan looked like the village he remembered. When he had come before, during the Fascist terror, shutters had covered all the windows of the shops and houses. Shutters covered the windows tonight. But he saw light through the slats of the shutters. Lights showed through the curtains of second-floor windows. No weeds grew between the cobblestones. He smelled food cooking.

As he entered Azatlan, he heard music and a woman singing. The song rose and fell with the shifting of the wind. Notes echoed through the streets. Lyons walked through the moonlit village, passing voices and radios on both sides. Though he saw no one on the streets, that did not bother him. Central American villages closed after nine in the evening. But with luck, he would find an open pension. Maybe even a restaurant.

He followed the highway into the town square. There the song echoed in the deserted but brilliantly lighted square. Pausing, he scanned the transformation. Before, bullet scars had marked the church. Now the church glowed with whitewash. Before, only merc and phony army vehicles were parked on the cobblestones. Now he saw the poles and awnings of vendors' stalls along the promenade. Fading Feliz Nuevo Año decorations hung on the fountain.

Across the square he saw light in the window of the police station. Whitewash and a Cervesa Gallo ad covered a wall where his Konzak assault shotgun had sprayed the blood and flesh of two men. Gray sandbags shielded the door of the police station—but Lyons knew that to be the rule in Guatemala, not an exception.

Light came from another doorway. A restaurant? Cantina? The music came from there. He had not eaten anything since the meal on the airplane. Hungry, Lyons hurried across the square and stepped inside.

He immediately regretted it.

4

Soldiers crowded the café.

Lyons continued three steps inside before stopping in midstride. For an instant his head pivoted, scanning the interior—the five tables, the cassette player, the Christmas tree and the blinking lights, the squad of camouflage-uniformed soldiers in berets, the Galil rifles on the tables and leaning against the chairs.

The clutter of beer bottles and the two open bottles of *aguardiente*, the clear, tasteless eighty-proof drink of the highlands.

The alcohol-glazed eyes of teenagers fixed on him.

As his movement and the weight of his pack carried him forward, ending his instant of too-late recon, he worked out the numbers of the situation:

An unknown number of empty beer bottles.

Two almost-empty one-liter bottles of eighty-proof corn alcohol.

Ten drunken Guatemalan teenagers.

Ten Galil automatic rifles in 5.56mm. Every rifle set on full-auto. One tall blond stranger who did not look like a tourist.

Lyons decided to act nonchalant. If Gadgets had been there, he would have said, "Be cool. And maybe they'll be cool, too."

A middle-aged ladino washed dishes in the back room. Lyons leaned over the counter—he knew every soldier in the café watched him—and called out in his best guidebook Spanish, "Good evening. Are you serving dinner?"

The ladino stared at him for a moment, as if not believing whom he saw. Finally he answered with a wave of his soapy hand. "Here's the menu...."

Lyons looked at the menu on the wall. In his peripheral vision he saw the teenagers watching him. It was a very basic menu offering steak, chicken and eggs, served with beans, cheese and tortillas. Steak or chicken for about $1.98. Eggs for $1.32. Beer and soda pop to drink, for fifty cents and seventeen cents.

Behind him, a teenager laughed. Lyons just grinned and asked the man. "I want a steak and—" he began.

"There's no steak. The soldiers took them all."

"Do you have any chicken?"

"No. The soldiers—"

"Eggs?—"

"Yes."

"Beer?"

The man nodded, and Lyons ordered eggs and beer.

The ladino wiped off his hands and went to the stove. Lyons turned and looked for a table. Soldiers and Galil rifles occupied every table.

One soldier who looked two or three years older than the rest and wore a black beret instead of the standard camo-patterned cap motioned to two soldiers. They nodded and left a table. The soldier in the black beret—Lyons saw two brass bars of rank, a second lieutenant?—made eye contact with Lyons. Lyons gave him a casual salute and started for the open table.

"You soldier?" a voice asked.

Lyons cursed himself. Why couldn't you have said thank-you like a tourist? Turning, Lyons said, "No, sir. Not me."

Then his pack caught the corner of a table.

Beer bottles shattered, the stamped-steel of galils clattered, chairs scraped back. In the kitchen a frying pan clanged. Soldiers laughed.

The lieutenant motioned for Lyons to continue to his table as the soldiers picked up their autorifles. Soldiers near the counter pointed and called out to their friends. They pointed to the middle-aged man who had dropped the frying eggs that had landed on the floor. With cautious dignity the ladino returned to cooking the tourist's dinner.

As Lyons unbuckled his hip belt and the across-the-chest tension strap he felt someone grip the back of the pack. The lieutenant joined Lyons. "I tell soldier help you. Are you tourist... *o un vendedor? Su mochela—*"

The weight of the pack made the soldier stagger. Another soldier grabbed the pack. Together, laughing and wrestling with the weight, the two soldiers placed the pack on the table Lyons had accidentally cleared of bottles. The lieutenant sat down across from Lyons.

"Tourists no come here. You are tourist or who? You not hippie. You beard short...."

"Just a tourist. Missed my bus. Had to walk to town. Maybe I'm lost."

"Your passport, please." The lieutenant held out his hand.

As he gave the officer his passport, Lyons noted the young lieutenant's high-octane breath. Drunk. A second lieutenant stationed out in the sticks with no one but his squad to drink with at night. Be cool. He's checking me out to kill time. This could be easy, or this could be a very serious problem.

And no matter what, don't mention Nate.

"Pardon me, it is my duty. I check strangers who travel. Please open your backpack."

Leaning across to the other table, Lyons pulled first one zipper then the other around to the bottom of the pack. He flipped back the flap to expose the interior.

"Oh, you from United States, Mr. Stone. Very good." The lieutenant called out to the café owner. *"Dos mas cervezas, inmediamente!* We will be very good friends, Mr. Stone. I am Alfredo." Then the Guatemalan spoke a phrase he had learned from North American television. "Have a tall cold one."

And the ladino put the beer down in front of Lyons. The document check became a search of the gifts. Lieutenant Alfredo bought Lyons another beer as he waited for his eggs and tortillas. When the soldiers found the cassette tapes, Alfredo glanced at the rhythm-and-blues and jazz titles and smiled.

"We play. Regulations, Señor Stone."

Three beers on an empty stomach had restored Lyons's bravado. "Why? Think they're Communist propaganda?"

Lieutenant Alfredo nodded gravely. "Perhaps it is a secret system. International Communist communication. We capture some Communists with tapes."

"But the tapes have still got the factory wrapper." Lyons gulped the last of the second beer. The lieutenant signaled for another. "American companies don't record for Communists."

"You do know of the Jefferson Airplane? Communists! We must play tapes. Regulations. All *norteamericano* rock 'n' roll and jazz we play. *Cassettas mexicanas,* no. I very tired of *mexicana* music."

Listening to Miles Davis, Lyons finished most of the third beer before the café owner brought the dinner.

The eggs had no taste. The beans looked like black soup spilled on the plate. The stale, hard tortillas had been burned. Lyons wondered if the cheese had been pasteurized. Lieutenant Alfredo laughed.

"There are good restaurants in the capital. But there are no good meals here—"

Calculating the protein value against the expected taste of the food, Lyons broke the tortillas and used the hard fragments like corn chips to eat the eggs and beans. He decided to look for food in the market the next day. Fresh tortillas, avocados, broiled meat, maybe some fruit. He would not eat at this café again.

A bottle of *aguardiente* appeared in front of him. "Here, here," a soldier told him. "Here is the sauce for your dinner. It is very delicious."

"It is truth, *norteamericano.*" Lieutenant Alfredo told him. The lieutenant took glasses off another table. He filled one for himself, another for Lyons. "After food, drink. You forget food."

Two glasses of *aguardiente* later, Lyons tried to pay the bill. The café owner had gone to sleep in the kitchen. Lyons put some quetzales in one of the kitchen drawers. He found himself weaving as he returned to his table. The lieutenant gave him a salute.

"You clean, *norteamericano*. Not subversive. But we play your *cassettas* tonight. Why you no carry *Playboy* magazines? Or *Penthouse*?"

Lyons closed up his pack. He noted the tapes the soldiers had at the cassette player.

The lieutenant continued his interrogation. "Tell me truth. Why you come here? No pyramids here. No water ski. No girls. The papas kill you with machete if you make out with the girls. This bad, bad place. Why you come?"

"A bus driver told me this was a shortcut to Coban."

"A shortcut? There is no shortcut! The road...here it stop. Only mountains."

"Then I stop here, too."

The lieutenant did not accept his answers. "Tell me truth! Why you come here? Tell! Or I make you tell...."

All the other soldiers, except those who had passed out on the floor, watched their lieutenant question the foreigner. Lieutenant Alfredo glanced to his men. He motioned for two soldiers to stand behind Lyons. That denied him any chance of a sprint out the door. The lieutenant took out a long rusty knife from a belt sheath.

"You think I not make you talk? You think I not torture? You no read books of Amnesty International? Tell me! Or..." The lieutenant leaned close to make his threat, "I make you stay here and eat breakfast."

Laughing, the lieutenant detailed the horrors of his threat. "More eggs! More beans! More tortillas!"

Lyons drank another glass of *aguardiente*. His years as a detective with the Los Angeles police and as a specialist fighting in the hellfires of the terrorist wars had introduced him to the realities of Third World wars. As a specialist, he moved fast. He found his target, killed it, then got out.

The lieutenant and his teenage squad represented a different view of the hellgrounds, garrison duty, the day-to-day routine of watching the roads and hills for movement, seeing the same villagers, the same truck drivers, checking the same identification day after day, the unrelenting boredom of waiting for a guerrilla with a grenade to come and throw it.

But here, the war had ended. Two years before, Nate and Able Team had wiped out the mercenary army. And throughout the nation, the Guatemalan army and the new civil-patrol system had decimated the rebels. Lieutenant Alfredo did not even have the thrill of a guerrilla attack to anticipate.

Lyons wondered what the lieutenant knew of the mercenaries who had occupied the region. So he chanced a conversation about the war.

"So how's hunting? Shoot any Communists lately?"

"No. Not for a month. And that one was a bad one. All bones. No good to eat."

The lieutenant laughed for a minute at his own joke. Then he continued. "The war is over. It is good now. Secure."

"Then why are you here? Why soldiers if it's okay now?"

"It cheap here. *Muy barato!* Very good to keep soldiers here. *El capital* very expensive. Understand?"

"Makes sense."

"But it's no fun!" Slapping his hand down on the table, Lieutenant Alfredo declared, "No pyramids. No water ski. No fun. Maybe we find guerrillas. Come, Señor Stone. We hunt guerrillas. Maybe we find a fat one for breakfast! Drink! Drink! Then we go!"

The high altitude and alcohol combination created flashes of scenes in Lyons's memory of the night.

He remembered the troop truck bumping over the dirt roads, horn blaring, searchlight waving over brush and stone walls. His backpack hung upside down, the hip belt looped through the slat sides, and he hung on to the pack for security.

A flare arced into the sky and burst. Lyons's eyes skipped. He could not focus on the flare descending beneath the miniature parachute. But one of the soldiers managed to aim his Galil and fire out a magazine of tracers, the line of bullets rising hundreds of yards above them into the night sky, never falling, burning out in the darkness, seeming to become stars.

Cornfields swayed and rippled with the wind as the truck's headlights swept around curves.

In another scene a dog ran alongside the truck barking, finally appearing in the red light of the taillights. Lyons felt the cold metal of a Galil in his hands. Forgetting to hide his familiarity with the autorifle, he did not snap-aim and jerk the trigger.

He flipped up the tritium-bead night sights, then clicked the fire-selector lever up from full-auto to semi. He braced his left shoulder against the slat sides and let his hands float with the lurching of the truck.

The single shot went through the dog from the nose to the asshole, flipping the animal backward into the darkness.

Lyons palmed the fire-selector lever up to safe before returning the rifle to a soldier.

Lieutenant Alfredo had watched. Leaning close to Lyons, he shouted over the laughter and jokes and the noise of the truck.

"You're no tourist."

5

Banging woke Lyons.

Lyons opened his eyes to darkness. Points of light sparkled in front of his face. Every breath he took smelled of oil and old dust. He tried to move but his hands remained still.

He kicked wildly and white light seared his eyes. He felt cold air in his throat.

Something was knotted around his throat. He grabbed it, struggling against the knot.

A blanket.

Blankets covered him. Had the soldiers dumped him in a bed somewhere? Or a rag pile?

Throwing off the blankets, he squinted against brilliant sunlight. The banging continued.

A hangover? Did his pulse bang like that? He heard laughter.

His eyes finally adjusted to the daylight. He lay in a tangle of blankets in the back of the troop truck. Above him, leaning over rows of gray plastic sandbags, two soldiers watched him and laughed.

Whitewashed walls enclosed a courtyard jammed with parked trucks. Soldiers occupied sandbag positions on the walls, their chairs tilted back, their feet resting on machine guns. One soldier used an empty sandbag and the extended legs of a Galil bipod to make a steel and gray plastic sunshade.

More laughter came from behind the truck. Nate and the lieutenant watched him and laughed. A soldier with them beat on the steel bumper of the truck with an ax handle.

"What are you doing here?" Nate demanded.

"I'm on vacation. I wrote you that I'd be—"

"Didn't you get my telegram?"

"No, when did you send it?"

"Forget it, spookman. You're here now. Get your gear."

The lieutenant questioned Nate quickly in Spanish. Lyons did not understand any of the conversation. Nodding, the lieutenant finally turned to Lyons.

"Why you no tell me? You friend? I think you CIA— Understand? *CIA*."

"I understand," Lyons answered. "Not me. I'm not one of them."

"No, man. Not you."

The same Nate. The thick-necked, barrel-chested marine, AWOL from a career in Leavenworth. His black hair, high cheekbones and a high-altitude tropical tan made him look like an *indígena*. The long-ago smashing of his nose concealed that detail of his non-Quicherno genetics.

Though he had cut his hair short and wore store-bought clothes, Nate did not look like a man of sudden wealth. His clothes had faded and frayed from washings on creek stones. He wore the sandals of an *indígena*. And Lyons recognized the same knit bag with the figure of a prancing horse hanging on Nate's shoulder.

Now the bag carried a cloth-wrapped bundle. Before, Nate had used the bag to carry loaded magazines for his G-3 sniper rifle.

Lyons dropped to the dirt of the street, then pulled down his heavy pack. He staggered a few steps as he slipped the straps over his shoulders.

"You on vacation?" Nate demanded. "Or are you moving here? You look like Santa Claus came late."

"You're talking to the man himself. Mr. Santa Claus. Ask Alfredo what I got in here."

"Good things! Rock 'n' roll!"

Nate said something to the Guatemalan in Spanish. Laughing, the lieutenant slapped the pack and shoved Lyons toward the gate of the compound.

Soldiers waved to Lyons. Looking around at the sandbagged walls, Lyons counted three old Browning 30-caliber machine guns. The 1921 air-cooled model that fired the obsolete, but very lethal 30-06 round.

"Guess I was safe last night."

Nate glanced at the teenagers on the walls. "This is the most dangerous place I know of. None of these punks knows that a safety can be set anywhere but full-automatic."

"I noticed."

"And you would have noticed if they had one of their accidents with grenades." Nate waited until a soldier closed the compound gate behind them before saying, "I sent you a telegram telling you to stay away. There's a pickup out in an hour and you ought to go."

"What's happened?"

Nate did not answer immediately. He glanced both directions in the wide street. A half block away, Lyons saw *indígenas*—Quicheneras in the *traje* of two different pueblos—selling fruit and vegetables in front of the church.

"Nothing. Nothing happened."

"Then why you want me to go?"

"Things are strange."

"Then maybe you need me to be here."

"Oh yeah. I need someone who can't talk Castilian. Can't talk *Q'ui che'*—" Nate pronounced the name of the language with the correct guttural sounds. "I need some blond blue-eyed spook that walks around with Christmas in his backpack and gets drunk and shoots dogs."

Lyons laughed. "They had ten Galils. When the second lieutenant said, 'Drink,' I drank."

"And if something happens, you won't have any high-technology backup. I think you ought to go. Come back when I don't have Salvadorans asking about me at the bank."

"That's what happened?"

Nate nodded.

"But nothing here?"

"That was in the capital. I lost them. There won't be any problems here."

"When you go there again, I'll go with you."

"You volunteering?"

"Why not? But right now, I want to get some food. Haven't eaten, not real food since I left Washington."

"If you can wait a couple of hours, we'll be back at my place for lunch."

"I got to have something now! You got a car here? You buy a car with the money? I want to lock up this bagful of toys."

"The cooperative bought a truck, there—" Nate pointed to a battered ten-year-old GMC pickup parked at the other side of the street. "You don't need to lock anything. No one will steal from me."

"All these teenagers," Lyons said, glancing at the soldiers on the wall, "know I've got cassette tapes in here."

"Ah, yeah...we'll lock up the pack."

After Lyons put the backpack in the cab, Nate found keys in his knit bag and locked the doors. They walked to the square.

Despite the brilliant morning it was cold in the shadows. Lyons found his sunglasses in one of his jacket pockets and walked in the morning sunlight. Wind brought the scents of burning wood and meat.

"So what's life been like out here?" Lyons finally asked.

"In the last few months, good. Since the fighting stopped."

"What fighting? You mean the Uno mercs?"

Nate glanced to Lyons, his eyes narrowed against the glare. "There was a war here. It may not have been in the newspapers, but there was a war. Unomundo was only one part of it. We still have squads of the EG wander into the valley."

"The Ejercito de los Pauves?"

"Your Spanish is getting better. I almost understood that. Yeah, them. Rich punks from the city who want our people to join the army of the people and die for the revolution, so the rich punks can be the new *caudillos*."

"And I thought they were Communists."

"Who knows?" They neared the first vendors. "We can't talk about that anymore. Someone might misunderstand. Now we talk food. What do you want?"

Lyons saw a woman stirring a kettle of meat and vegetable soup. "That—" A few steps farther, another woman sold several varieties of bananas—yellow, red and plantains. "And those, and—"

Passing some coins to the woman, Nate took a spoon and a steaming bowl of the soup. Lyons scooped out and gulped down the vegetables. He had difficulty chewing the tough meat. Nate bought a handful of *tamalitas*—corn dough baked in folded banana leaves—and gave those to Lyons. Lyons squatted on the church steps and set the bowl on the stones, freeing his left hand to cram *tamalitas* in his mouth.

"Didn't think you'd like pig intestines," Nate commented.

Lyons stopped chewing. He looked at the bowl. He swallowed. Then he ate the last of the pig *menudo* and drank the dregs of the bowl. "Didn't think I'd like pig guts, either. Where can I buy a steak?"

"People around here can't afford beef. Maybe beef guts."

"Chicken?"

Nate grinned. "You'll eat a chicken, alive? You must be hungry."

"What about a cooked chicken?"

"People don't eat a chicken unless it dies. Go to a restaurant if you want—"

"Forget it. Did that last night. How about those avocados? And where can I get some tortillas?"

As they passed along the row of vendors, Nate stopped to talk with a man. They spoke in *Quiche*. For a moment Lyons stood at the side and watched the conversation he could not understand. Then he signaled Nate that he would continue looking for food.

Jingling a handful of coins, Lyons went to a woman who sold bananas. He squatted in front of the pile. Pointing to a stalk of the small red variety, he asked how much.

The woman looked to her companions, her dark eyes moving like a lizard's in the mahogany-colored mask of her face. He heard her friends speaking in *Quiche*. He recognized only the words "quetzal" and "centavos."

"Un quetzal cada," she told him.

One quetzal each! Lyons rocked back on his heels, faking absolute shock. The group of women laughed, their weathered faces opening in smiles that revealed bad teeth. Lyons again asked the price.

"Diez centavos cada." Ten cents each, and this time the woman did not laugh. But around her, the other women laughed.

Lyons gave her a hard look. He offered a ten-centavo coin and held up three fingers. Again the women laughed. The *vendedora* snatched three bananas off the stalk and grabbed the coin.

The other vendors around him called out, offering him avocados, a clucking chicken, a *huipile*, tortillas, a pig's head. He realized he had paid too much.

But it ain't a serious mistake, he rationalized. Six point six cents for three bananas.

He slipped out his knife, the phosphate-black blade like a shadow in his hand, and he held up the bananas to cut off the stems.

The banana vendor started. Sneaking a glance to her associates, she rolled her eyes in mock fear. She offered him a tiny five-centavo coin. The others laughed as she put her hands together as if praying and repeated, *"Perdóneme, señor."*

Lyons shook his head and slashed off the banana stems. Using the point of the blade, he drew long cuts down the bananas, then flicked off the slices of skin. The bananas had a different taste, like a cross between strawberries and bananas. He had eaten similar bananas a few months before in Sri Lanka. He gulped each banana in two bites.

"Basura?" He held up the handful of banana peels. The women laughed and laughed. The banana vendor dared to reach past the black knife and Lyons gave her the peels. She threw the peels on the stones. While the vendors laughed Lyons realized that the entire street served as a trash can.

He continued to the next vendor and bargained for tortillas. Not understanding the woman, he continued the negotiations, offering a few centavos more in each reply.

Abruptly, the old *indígena* nodded and took his money. She reached into her cloth-wrapped bundle and took out a six-inch stack of tortillas. Holding up a chain-and-balance-bar scale, she weighed the tortillas. She took off three and wrapped the stack in a banana leaf.

A kilo. He had bought a kilo of corn tortillas. Did he want to eat 2.2 pounds of corn dough for breakfast?

Twenty-five centavos bought two avocados. He continued past the displays until he found another soup vendor. Sitting down on the curb next to the fire, he spread out the banana leaf across his legs and cut open an avocado. He put a big slab of avocado on a tortilla.

He offered ten centavos to the ancient woman stirring a pot and asked, "Meat?"

Nodding, she searched the soup, then dropped a length of gray boiled flesh on the tortilla. Lyons gave the meat a quick glance, then covered it with another tortilla.

Most definitely intestine.

Eating the *menudo* sandwich, he watched the people talking and joking about him. He ate four more sandwiches before Nate rejoined him.

"So what's going on?" Lyons asked.

"He will tell me if any strangers come to the village."

Nate sat down next to Lyons. He took a handful of tortillas and ate them. Past the village square, over the low roofs, clouds swept over the forested mountains. The two men ate tortillas and watched the swirling clouds.

The vendors around them called out to one another, the jokes continuing. Lyons asked Nate, "What are they saying?"

"Just talk and jokes. They got nothing else to do. A foreigner comes to town and eats and it's an event. So they joke and laugh."

Taking another tortilla, Nate cut a slice of avocado. He studied the black blade for a moment, then mashed the avocado on the tortilla like spreading butter.

"Now, me. I'm different. I live here eight years. I wear the clothes. I speak the language. I got a local wife, two kids. They see me all the time. I'm one of them. Now they only make jokes at me when they got nothing else to do."

6

Two gringos....

Captain Gonzalez of the national police watched the two *norteamericanos* through the viewfinder of the Nikon. They sat on the curb diagonally across the narrow street from the police station. Seen through the 150mm setting of the zoom lens, the men filled the viewing frame. The brilliant morning light sharply defined their features.

Awkward with the expensive camera, Gonzalez adjusted the focus of the lens. Perfect. He saw the morning light sparkling from the beard stubble of the blond stranger.

The intelligence officer in the capital—Gonzalez did not even know the man's office or rank, only the name Chino — had given the captain quick instruction in photography. The captain had experimented and practiced in the months since then. Now he knew what to do to get useful identification photos.

He crouched at a second-floor window of the police station, only the lens extending through the curtains. The gringos would not see him photographing them. With the lens resting on the plaster of the windowsill, Gonzalez knew he had the option of a slow exposure. Perhaps one sixtieth of a second.

Watching the exposure meter needle at the left side of the viewing frame, he flicked on the camera's power. The green needle hit the top of the scale, faster than one-thousandt of a second. Gonzalez glanced at the f-stop window above the image frame—f3.5.

He felt for the aperture ring and twisted it two clicks to f5.6. The needle wavered on one thousand. Another twist closed the aperture down to f8. The needle fell to five hundred. Gonzalez went two clicks farther, to f16. The needle floated on 125. Perfect.

Checking the focus, he watched the blond gringo shoving tortillas into his face like a bestial *indígena,* worse even than the pretender eating next to him. Gonzalez questioned the sanity of the man he knew was called Nate. That *norteamericano* had given up life in the United States to live as a Quichenero in the mountains, to rut with an *indígena* bitch and make ignorant children.

Insane. A drug-damaged criminal. Chino, the intelligence officer, had told Gonzalez the *norteamericano* committed several crimes in the north, escaped prison, then fled south to Guatemala, where he thought the law would never follow. Did he think Guatemala had no laws, no police? The *norteamericano* authorities, with their computers and laboratories and jets, had not found that brain-diseased creature. In the end only the hard work of Guatemalans tracked him down.

And this other criminal, why had he come to Azatlan? Gonzalez knew his photos would aid in the investigation and the arrests. Would he receive credit? Promotion from this dirty town in the mountains? A reward from the wealthy gringo authorities?

Gonzalez snapped photo after photo, thumbing the film winder in jerks, stopping to check the focus each time. When the men stood, he snapped photos faster, recording their faces from the slightly different angle. The last exposures showed the two men walking away.

Carefully rewinding the film, he popped the roll from the camera. He replaced the camera in its aluminum case and locked the case in his office. Then he telephoned the number of an army office in Huehuetenango.

As he had the other times during the months of surveillance, he would make the two-hour drive to the west and personally deliver the roll of film to a soldier parked at the side of the Pan-American Highway.

The film would be in the capital before nightfall.

7

Winding dirt roads led into the mountains. Despite the age of the cooperative's GMC pickup, Nate maintained a steady speed over the ruts and small stones. Lyons watched the landscape change from sloping fields, to mountains, then to black volcanic cliffs cut by pine-forest ravines. As they gained altitude, the wind came in gusts that rocked the truck. Wind-driven clouds seemed to smash into the vertical cliff faces and shatter into white fragments of mist.

Working the gears and clutch with the changes in grade, Nate talked in laconic sentences. He briefed Lyons on the changes in the two years since Able Team had fought there.

The destruction of Unomundo's base and mercenary army had not brought peace to Azatlan.

"Killing those thousand psychos did not stop the shit. People came back to the town. Came back to their fields. But the war came with them.

"The psycho-mercs kept the RG away. With the mercs gone, EG units came down out of the mountains. They hit army and police units. They would ambush them and then retreat through the valley. We'd have running firefights and air strikes every few weeks."

The tires threw gravel against the fenders, and Nate shouted over the noise. "The army set up a garrison—you were in there. Sent out patrols to find the EG. The colonel had been one of Unomundo's Nazis—goddamned *puto* traitor—and he tried to question people about what happened. Many questions. But no one talked.

"Then one of our men made a mistake. He went hunting with an M-16 we had taken from the Unos. He got caught and questioned. The colonel knew the EG didn't have M-16s so he really put it to our fellow. Took it for three days, finally died. He did not talk. Then that *puto* colonel took it out on his family, butchered them.

"So Colonel Puto disappeared...." Nate turned to Lyons. "You understand?"

Lyons nodded. And he knew that the colonel would never reappear.

"The colonel who replaced him was much different," Nate continued. "Loyal to the government. He did not know what had happened out here. He only wanted to hunt the EG and set up the civil-patrol units to fight the international Communist conspiracy.

"He had village assemblies. Set up loudspeakers. Preached 'beans and bullets.' The duty of the people to the nation. The evil of neutrality. The evil of communism. Promised schools and electricity. New roads. Should have saved his breath.

"Everyone knew the facts. Fight or get shit on.

"We formed the civil patrols. We carried the old worn-out Mausers the army issued and when we spotted the EG, we pulled some evil maneuvers.

"We popped a few shots at them. Get their attention. Those Fidel boys would chase our patrols, thinking they'd have fire superiority when they caught us. Their M-ls and Galils against our bolt-action Mausers. And we'd have twenty or thirty men waiting in an ambush, with the weapons we took from Unomundo. M-16s, M-60s, M-79s.

"We'd chop up the bodies with machetes so no one could count the wounds, then bring out the army to look at the pieces. After the machetes and the dogs, no one could tell what happened to them."

"Dogs?" Lyons interrupted. "The dogs around here eat people?"

"That's one of the reasons there's such a problem with wild dogs. So much killing in the last few years."

"Yeah, well, it was me they tried to eat last night."

Nate shrugged and continued. "The generals thought that the colonel was magic. The colonel got a promotion. Got transferred back to the capital. Now he spends all his time preaching civil patrols on television. Like it was a new religion. Like an evangelist. And now we get college dropout lieutenants like Alfredo. Who are no problem at all."

"But what about the money?" Lyons finally asked. "You bought this truck. Correction, you said the cooperative bought the truck. What're you doing with that hundred grand? You didn't give it all to some cooperative, did you?"

Nate guided the truck around a hairpin turn. "You didn't pay the money to me. You paid it to everyone who was in the assault on the cave, and to the families of the men who didn't come back. All of us formed the cooperative. It's a working organization now."

"Wow, sounds like socialism to me."

"So what? Call it what you want."

"But what did you buy?"

"We got a bank."

With the noise of rocks banging the fenders, Lyons hadn't heard Nate. "You put it in a bank?"

"No. We made a bank. Does that sound like socialism? A bank for all of us out here. A cooperative fund. We borrow money from the bank and then pay it back. When a child gets sick, we don't need to sell our land to buy medicine. The men don't go to the coast to work on the coffee plantations. Used to go four months a year, leave their families alone while they're gone for months. EG and mad-dog colonels running loose in the valley and the men are gone. But not any more. That hundred thousand gave us a chance at the twentieth century."

"Why you saying 'we'? Did you actually pick coffee?"

"Yeah. Years ago. Before the war. War came and they started checking identification too close. Except that I needed that money; I didn't regret picking coffee. Bad life on those *fincas*. Sometimes men don't come back. Accidents. Some men die of the insecticide. Bosses suspect you of organizing a union, or talking about a union, or listening to another man talk about a union, you are dead. But now we're all past that. We can stay with our families. Work our land, save our money."

"Finally," Lyons said. "Foreign aid that did something for someone—"

"What are you talking about? Foreign aid? Don't make me laugh. Foreign aid goes to the rich. We fought for that money. Ramon and Francisco Cael, they were the ones that got captured, they died for that money. Salvador Mendoza and Oscar Sax fought and died. Juan Saquic drags his left leg because he took a merc's bullet through the knee.

"The Creoles in the capital pay off a few congressmen, give them a good time with some hundred-dollar whores and they get highways and import quotas. Don't even say that shit, foreign aid."

"Don't lecture me. I know."

"How could you know? You read it in the newspaper?"

"I see it."

Nate glanced at the hard-eyed ex-cop. "I forget. You go there. Yeah, spookman. You're okay. You're not even a spookman."

"Then why do you call me 'spookman'?"

"I want to, that's why." Nate laughed.

"Did you at least use some of the money to finish your house?"

"You'll see...."

After two hours on the roads Lyons did see. The final stretch of dirt track cut across a plateau. Weaving through a pine forest, the road passed wild-flower meadows planted with rectangles of corn. A teenager in the *traje* of the pueblo, and an ancient Mauser carbine slung over his back, watched a flock of sheep. Lyons recognized the young man.

"¿Xagil!" Lyons shouted from the truck. "What's happening?"

"¿Spookman!"

His red-and-yellow woven pants splashing through the high grass, Xagil ran to the truck. Nate sped up, leaving the teenager behind, forcing him to sprint to grab the tailgate and pull himself over. Xagil held on to the cab's roof and looked through the rear window at Lyons.

"Santa Claus is coming to town," Lyons joked to Nate.

A hundred yards farther, the pines stopped and the plateau seemed to fall into blue sky. Only a wire-mesh fence remained between the truck and space. Nate braked.

The AWOL marine had finished his dream house. Built only a few steps back from a thousand-foot fall, the house had thick adobe walls to insulate the interior from the cold winds. Heavy timbers framed the doorways and windows. One large window gave a view of the valley. A roof of pressed-asbestos corrugated sheets sheltered the interior from the tropical sun and the torrential rains.

Lyons noted that Nate had not whitewashed the sunbaked adobe walls. Pine saplings had been planted where they could arch over the house. And patterns of black and gray paint splotched the corrugated asbestos roof.

Camouflage. Not a decor featured in *Better Homes and Gardens*, but appropriate for a house in mountains where the Ejercito Guerrilla de los Pauves, Fascist *desconocidos*, and apolitical bandits fought for supremacy. A house two hours by truck from the nearest office of law enforcement.

As Lyons left the cab of the truck Xagil jumped out of the back. The teenager tried to pull out Lyons's backpack. Xagil strained, he gasped, then Lyons leaned over the side of the truck and lifted the pack straight up. He looped one strap over his shoulder and lurched toward the house.

When Nate emerged from the truck, he had an Uzi in one hand, a bandolier of magazines in the other. Lyons had not even seen the submachine gun in the truck. Nate handled the weapon with the casual ease of day-to-day familiarity, opening the door to his home and hanging the Uzi and ammunition over a hook at the side of the door.

Galils, a G-3 and an M-79 grenade launcher already hung on the rack.

"Expecting problems?" Lyons asked.

"No," Nate said, then continued, "Dogs have been getting our chickens. You ready for another meal?"

"Great! And after lunch I open up the pack."

In *Quiche*, Nate called out to his wife. She emerged from a doorway across the large central room. As she had two years before, she wore the traditional clothes of her pueblo, a hand-woven red-and-purple *huipile* and a black full-length skirt. Again, she held an infant, Nate's second child, Quetzal. His son Tecun hid behind his mother.

Marylena greeted Lyons with a nod. Lyons saw Marylena's widowed older sister—Xagil's mother—behind her. Nate and the women spoke quickly in *Quiche* and Spanish, then the women left. Lyons heard Marylena calling out to Xagil.

Nate gave Lyons a tour of the house. "This is our side of the house. There's my picture window. Always wanted one. That's the kitchen. That door goes to her sister's side. Xagil's got a room over there.

You'll sleep here. Sun coming through the picture window will wake you up. No indoor bathroom yet. No electricity. No television.''

"But you got this great view...." Lyons stared out the long window. A few miles away, smoke rose from the village of Azatlan. The green-and-brown patchwork of fields, cut by the lines of asphalt and dirt roads, extended into the distance. Perhaps thirty miles away, feathery smoke rose from another village hidden by forest. The panorama included three mountain ranges, the third line of peaks only a gray line against the blue of the sky.

He realized the window had three six-foot-by-four-foot sheets. "How did you get this glass up here?"

"The truck. Broke four sheets to get those three up here."

Outside chickens clucked, then squawked, then came the death squawks. Nate smiled.

"Lunch," he said.

After a meal of *mole pablano*—chicken cooked in chocolate sauce, young corn, squash, steamed snap beans and the ever-present tortillas—Lyons finally opened his pack.

He took out an NSA solar-panel battery charger for Nate, to power his Sony multiband shortwave radio; walkie-talkies that Lyons had smuggled past customs concealed in his spare shoes; cassette players for Marylena and Xagil; North American rhythm-and-blues and jazz—the cassettes tested by the soldiers—for Nate; an eclectic selection of tapes for the family, including folk songs, Mexican ballads, music of Peruvian flutes and Guatemalan xylophones, American and English rock; rechargable miniflashlights; black cordura boots, like the boots Lyons wore, for Nate; brilliant-red running shoes for Xagil; Italian clear-plastic sandals for Nate's wife and sister-in-law; cartoon characters with glow-in-the-dark eyes for Nate's three-year-old boy, Tecun; a spectrum of fruit flavored and scented felt-tip markers for Tecun and maybe for the infant Quetzal if the markers lasted another year; a brightly colored plastic mobile of birds to hang above Quetzal's crib; and a spectrum of furry baby pajamas for Quetzal.

After the gift-giving ceremony Lyons and Nate went outside to escape the cacophony of music and voices—Radio Free Europe, the Beatles and Julio Iglesias played all at once. Nate laughed as he opened two earth-cooled beers.

"You carried all that? You carried that up the hill last night?"

"All the way up the hill, all the way down."

Nate gulped beer. He turned to Lyons. "No more 'spookman.' Anyone who's got it to carry all that up a mountain can't have any kind of agency name."

"Just call me Ironman, as in 'legs of iron.'"

"Forget that. I'll call you anything I want, Santa."

8

Faces emerged from the processing machine.

The black-haired *norteamericano* sat on a curb beside the blond one. The exposure captured minutes of a conversation while they ate—smiles, silences, gestures with dripping tortillas, laughter. Then their backs as they walked away through the town's market.

Jose Alvarado, known as Chino to his ex-associates in the judicial police because he had served time in the State of California Correctional Facility at Chino, watched the color prints drop into the clear plastic bin. The rollers transported the last print to the bin and a switch clicked.

The vibrations of the motors stopped, but the whirring fans continued, cooling the interior of the French automatic-photo-processing machine. Taking the stack of warm prints to the work table, Chino spread out the images.

Outside the one-hour photo shop, evening traffic roared through the streets of Zone One of the capital of Guatemala. The noise came in surges as traffic signals released lines of trucks and cars and motorcycles to speed through the neon-lighted corridor of Sixth Avenue. When the traffic roar faded, Chino heard the music of teenagers cruising in their cars, beggars crying out, vendors shouting prices of wristwatches.

Chino surveyed the thirty-seven prints. Thirty-eight if he counted the light-slashed first frame of film. Gonzalez had learned quickly. Though the police commander had only an elementary-school education, he had overcome the difficulties of photography. In the months of ruined film, out of focus and underexposed shots, and tutoring through Chino's long notes from the photo shop, Gonzalez had not become a photographer, but he had finally succeeded in the most crucial test of all: he had seen the meeting of the *norteamericanos*, rushed to get the camera, then taken the photos—without a technical error that destroyed the exposures, without a surveillance error that would have alerted the *norteamericanos* to the continuing investigation.

Gonzalez had taken many repetitious exposures— the same facial angles, the same expressions—but Chino had encouraged the use of film.

"Film is very cheap," Chino had told him again and again. "The opportunity to photograph a suspect may come only once. Even if you waste one hundred rolls of film to take one good photo, that one photo may be the one we must have."

And Captain Gonzalez had taken four such photos.

One photo showed the profile of the blond *norteamericano* who had contacted the suspect.

Another showed a full frontal view of the contact man's face.

The next showed an angle of his face.

The last one showed the two men shoulder to shoulder, illustrating the difference in heights. With the three photos, there would be no mistake in the identification of the blond one. An artist could literally sculpt the man's head from those photos.

And the photo with the men walking side by side would fix the man's height within an error margin of one inch. The International knew the height of the man named Nate. Investigators would calculate the height of the contact man from the other information.

Chino put the negatives on the light box. With the magnifying lens, he studied the images, finding the correct negatives. He noted the frame numbers.

First, he fitted the negatives into the automatic machine and pressed the number 6 on the keyboard. The light inside the machine flashed six times, the motors automatically feeding print paper. In minutes he would have six duplicates each of the prints in the standard size. Then he went into the darkroom and made eight prints, all eight inches by ten inches, all in color.

He worked quickly. The sounds of the nightlife of the capital from outside reminded him of his date. He did not want his work to keep him from the young woman's apartment.

When the prints had dried he assembled two packages of photos.

One package of duplicate snapshots and four eight-by-ten prints would go to his superiors in the judicial police. The package would accompany the negatives and thirty-eight initial prints.

And, because the contact man seemed to be another U.S. citizen, more snapshots and four prints were to be air-expressed to the International's contacts in Washington, D.C., for identification.

On his motorcycle he went first to the offices of the judicial police, then across the city to the airport. The second set of photos went north on the next flight to the United States, for delivery to an office in Washington, D.C.

9

Sprawled on the black rocks, Lyons wore only his underwear and sunglasses. The unending atomic flare of the sun seared white in his closed eyes, the fifteenth-parallel noon burning his body. He sunbathed 125 miles closer to the equator than Acapulco and with 3,280 yards less of atmosphere between him and the sun.

A week of this, Lyons thought, and I'll be indigenized, a blond Quichenero.

He reached out blind and his hand found the one-liter bottle of *aguardiente*. Pouring the eighty-proof liquor into his mouth, he angled his head forward and sprayed out the vodka—clear firewater. The wind and the high-altitude low-pressure atmosphere flash-evaporated the alcohol, the spray cooling as it misted down on his body.

The thousands of droplets of liquor relieved the sun's heat. Lyons poured down a second mouthful and swallowed. Then a third mouthful.

Fire numbed his throat. The *aguardiente* burned to his stomach. But after a minute, the alcohol flowed through his blood, numbing the sense of the warm rocks under his back and legs. Then the fire of the *aguardiente* seemed to mix with the white fire within his eyes.

Lyons listened to the wind rushing past him. He lay on the black volcanic rocks overlooking the valley of Azatlan. Two or three steps past him, the black slabs sloped down to a vertical wall. The drop continued for a thousand feet to the pine forest below. Thermal updrafts rushed up the volcanic face in a sound like a continuing moan or an ecstatic sigh or a transcendental 'om.'

Crosswinds whistled through the pines behind him. The winds rushing over his body gave him the sensation of flight, as if he floated in the sky.

And when he opened his eyes, he saw only blue void and landscape, as if he flew through the sky.

The pleasure of the sun, the alcohol euphoria, illusion of flying.... This was a vacation!

Lyons took another gulp of *aguardiente*. A vacation meant no work. No Able Team missions against the psycho-political scum of the world.

Lying on his back in the sun, *aguardiente* within reach, his pleasure center on auto-cruise, Lyons felt no self-righteous loathing, no hatred of his enemies. Lists of names, crowds of faces flashed through his memory. Except for the few names and faces he knew to be past tense—dead, some maimed and imprisoned—they remained at freedom. Freedom to murder. To terrorize humanity. To splash blood over the earth.

So many of them. Like a two-thousand-page catalog of shit.

Unomundo, for one. In fact, at the top of the list. Somewhere in the world, the half-Hispanic/half-German would-be dictator plotted another move for the

Fascist International. Maybe against Guatemala. Maybe he planned the establishment of another drug gang in Mexico, where he didn't even need to recruit more gangs and technicians. Able Team had only killed a few soldiers of Los Guerros Blancos in Sonora and a few more in the TransAmericas tower of Mexico City. Maybe Able and the commandos of the Mexican Sixth army had inconvenienced the International's executives by wrecking their offices, but Lyons knew the firefight in the offices had not decapitated the leadership of the syndicates.

Unomundo could be anywhere now—in Mexico, in Miami, in Washington, D.C. or Manhattan—organizing another strike by the army of the International.

And Lyons was sprawled on a cliff in the Department of Quiche, Guatemala...trying for a serious tan.

Intellectually, he considered the guilt clouding his mind. He had to track down that Nazi supergoon and do A Serious Number On His Head!

Like an interocular injection of 150 number-two and double-0 steel balls at twelve hundred feet per second, that is, a full-auto 3-shot burst from his Konzak assault shotgun, point-blank to the blinking left eye of Klaust dc la Unomundo-Stiglitz, a.k.a. Miguel de la Unomundo. Then another burst to the right eye. A for-sure, most-definite lobotomy. Known also as a 12-gauge cephalodectomy.

Do the world a favor, pull a trigger on that Nazi. Don't stop at one trigger. Empty the weapon and use another one. Blister that trigger finger pulling triggers. Shoot him until someone calls for a street cleaner.

Lyons sat up, reaching for his clothes.

No time for vacations! No time to walk around in the moonlight and cry about dead friends. No time to see friends! No time to slop down booze and roll around in the sun! Lyons had some serious killing to do.

Unomundo had to die.

Lyons lay down again. Why should he feel that he should leave, go back to California or Washington and wait for the call? Why him?

The words of Talmud flashed through his mind:

If not me, who?
If not now, when?

Sorry, world. Later.

In fact, he did have a mission today. Sheepherding. Xagil had the commanding role in the job, but Lyons had his responsibilities, also. If any of the sheep fell over Lyons in a mindless wander toward the free-fall, Lyons had to stop the stupid creatures.

After all, Unomundo had friends watching out for him. Senators, congressmen, paid-off politicos in the White House. Lyons knew Unomundo bought American protection. The original mission against Unomundo started after the murder of two FBI agents. That chase led to Azatlan. After that Able Team went up against Salvadoran killers sent to murder refugees and Americans in the United States. Even though the evidence linked the death squads to Salvadoran friends of Unomundo, no one in Washington gave Able the go-ahead to pursue the link to the International. Finally, after six months, when a decent Salvadoran soldier came forth with information on Roberto Quesada, an International subcommander who had issued the commands to murder Americans, only then did Washington send Able Team south to El Salvador.

Into a trap.

Quesada had waited for them, his soldiers ready, an escape helicopter on the pad.

Able Team almost didn't come back from that mission.

And when a DEA investigation took them south again, to Sonora—only a few minutes from San Diego by plane—Unomundo's Washington friends had another surprise reception for their esteemed hotshots, an SAM missile.

If they hadn't had a twin-engine Lear jet, if they hadn't had an ace pilot, if they hadn't had the strength and training to march through the desert, avoiding squads of International soldiers, fighting through ambushes and turning them back on their pursuers....

Now Nate, he did not have that kind of protection for his sheep. He needed Lyons to guard this cliff. If a sheep went off the cliff, it meant that much less wool and meat for his family. From that perspective, lying in the sun—not sunbathing, but creating a human barricade against the stupidity of the walking hair balls—made sense.

Forget the world. Help your friends. Life's too short to be a do-gooder.

Except that he wanted Unomundo.

Lyons decided to put Unomundo on his red-ink list when he got back. In fact, at the moment, he did not have a red-ink list. But when he got back, after he had a few weeks of lying around in the sun and hiking through the forests of Quiche, he would most defi-

through the forests of Quiche, he would most definitely take a red marking pen and write the name *Unomundo* on poster paper. He would underline the Nazi name, then add the phrase, *Must Die*!

No doubt about it. First thing—when he got back.

In fact, maybe sooner. If Nate had been right, if he had actually spotted a surveillance team at his bank, Lyons might get into the act soon. Maybe next week. Lyons hoped it had been Nate's paranoia creating Fascist International gunmen in the bank's lobby. He did not want to go up against an organized force without his partners as backup. The fight could wait until he started it.

Until then, let the politicos of Washington keep banking the protection money of the International. The United States needed the dollars toward the balance-of-payments deficit. Lyons would have a good time while he could.

Because he knew one fact: he had gone against the International too many times already. He had lived through five missions against that particular gang. He had used up all his luck.

The next time....

He opened his eyes to the white light of the sun.

Death would be darkness for Carl Lyons, ex-cop, ex-husband, distant father, ex-lover of Flor Trujillo, ex-specialist.

But death could not touch his spirit, his life, the force that drove him through this world.

He knew it would happen. He accepted it.

Closing his eyes, he lay on the rocks and floated within the colors of the afterimage, praying he would be reborn in a place of beauty and peace.

10

An electronic beeping woke Alfonso Morales. Instantly awake, he left his bed in one motion. His hand snatched the beeper from his bedside table. Pressing the button to acknowledge the signal, he then took his perfectly folded slacks and shirt from the valet.

Though a political disaster had forced him to suddenly abandon his military career two years before, ex-Colonel Morales had not abandoned his lifelong habits of self-discipline and order. He dressed in less than ninety seconds. He compromised only on his shoes. Rather than taking another ninety seconds to lace shoes, he pushed his feet into his leather slippers and rushed from the bedroom.

Two years before, he had lost his commission, his name, his family and, he feared, his future. He had been one of many officers resolved to restore order in rebellion-torn Guatemala. They had argued among themselves, maneuvered against one another for power. Then a young man, younger than many of the officers, had appeared to lead them into the twenty-first century.

Miguel de la Unomundo offered the strongest, most determined men of the country a new future, a future merging military discipline and racial superiority with the logic of transnational corporate structure.

This young man had already made himself a billionaire. Starting with capital inherited from his father, a German expatriate who had served with the feared and glorious SS of the Third Reich, he multiplied his wealth through business acumen and ruthless suppression of competition. Nor did he tolerate unions or the legal regulations of petit bourgeois socialists and liberals.

Buying corporations, investing in urban real estate and farmland, Unomundo, who, proud of his Hispanic heritage, went by the name of his Castilian mother rather than his German father, became a multibillionaire. He donated vast sums of capital to conservative leaders everywhere in the western hemisphere and, in turn, they aided in the expansion of his business empire.

His interlocking corporations exploited every opportunity in the world, regardless of law—banks, shipping, air freight, drug plantations, chemicals, weapons factories, political parties, oil.

The Communist threat and the impotence of democracy created the opportunity for Unomundo to take Guatemala. For himself and the strong. He intended to seize Guatemala first, then the surrounding nations of Central America, then all other nations of the hemisphere. He declared his intentions so that none could misunderstand.

"A New Reich shall rise!"

Then came defeat. Unomundo's dream of a united hemisphere had been shattered by *norteamericano* assassins. Unomundo had survived, but he had abandoned—for a time—his dreams of the American Reich. The young genius devoted his energies to enriching his hundreds of corporations and rebuilding his military forces.

Morales had shared some of the guilt in that defeat, but Unomundo had not condemned him. Ex-Colonel Morales now enjoyed the life of a wealthy man.

True, Morales lost his commission in the army, but that had been inevitable. Unomundo immediately transferred Morales to the corporate offices of the transnational syndicates to generate the billions of dollars of cash needed by the International. And in his position as an executive, Morales earned hundreds of thousands of U.S. dollars for himself.

Instead of a small house in the middle-class suburbs, Morales now owned a sprawling mansion a halfhour by limousine from the capital.

Instead of the unending routine of military life, he now lived the life of a transnational executive, jetting throughout the world to fulfill his duties.

Instead of a fat wife and surly teenagers disrupting his life with their demands and pouts, he now enjoyed credit-card romances whenever his travel schedule allowed.

Not a bad life. But sometimes he wondered how he would have lived if Unomundo had been successful in his coup.

He would have had all this and more.

The plantation with the *indígena* slaves.

His private army.

And his command in the second conquest of the Americas.

Perhaps there would be another chance, he thought as he rushed across the mansion to his office. The beeper-signal meant an urgent message on his long-range electronically secured transceiver. Perhaps the rumors had come true.

The mobilization.

The beginning of the second conquest.

The extermination of the leftist contagion infecting Nicaragua, El Salvador and Mexico.

The liquidation of the leftist *norteamericanos* in the corrupt cities of the United States who would not join in the crusade for tradition and property.

The destruction of the petit bourgeois nations of the hemisphere, the liquidation of all the Communists, socialists, liberals and false conservatives who opposed the rise of the New Reich.

Punching the code of the electronic lock barring unauthorized entry to his office, Morales entered and saw green phosphor numbers glowing on the computer screen. The interlocked radio-computer had been manufactured by the United States National Security Agency and donated to the International. The computerized unit not only encoded messages entered by keyboard or microphone, but also transmitted the messages in high-speed screeches of electronic noise.

Even if the American NSA or the Society KGB or the Guatemalan Secret Service monitored the frequency, the communications might be mistaken for bursts of electronic disturbance from space.

Morales went to the keyboard and typed in his identification number and a sequence of acronyms reconfirming his identification. The acronyms provided additional security—in case of his capture and injection with will-suppressing drugs, the codes allowed him the opportunity to alert his commanders to his forced cooperation without committing suicide.

Seconds later, the text of the transmission appeared on the screen.

He read the instructions quickly, rage seizing his mind as the name appeared.

Carl Lyons, one of the *norteamericano* commandos who had stopped Unomundo's seizure of Guatemala, who had shattered the career of Colonel Morales, who had tortured his officers, who had murdered hundreds of his associates—Carl Lyons had come to Guatemala!

The commands he read next cooled his rage, gave his hatred a channel of execution. The message contained more than maddening information. The supreme military committee of the International graced him with a responsibility that offered Morales revenge for the defeat two years before:

ORGANIZE COMBAT SQUAD.

PROVIDE WEAPONS AND VEHICLES.

LIAISON OFFICERS WILL ARRIVE FROM HONDURAS WITHIN HOUR VIA TRANSAMERICAS S.A. PRIVATE JET. PROVIDE LIAISON OFFICERS WITH TRANSPORTATION FROM AIRPORT TO ASSEMBLY PLACE OF COMBAT TEAM.

ORDER SQUAD TO CAPTURE LYONS. REPEAT, CAPTURE. AT ANY COST.

INITIATE IMMEDIATE MOBILIZATION OF ARMY UNITS LOYAL TO INTERNATIONAL. ARMY OF GUATEMALA WILL CLOSE AREA AROUND LYONS WHILE COMBAT SQUAD SEARCHES:

COLONEL GUNTHER WILL ASSUME COMMAND OF SEARCH.

Though Morales had wanted to command the search and capture himself, the name of Colonel Gunther alerted him to the extreme importance the International placed on the capture of the *norteamericano*.

Colonel Gunther served as director of security for the International. He directed the units responsible for the personal security of Unomundo himself. The colonel also executed the special-action missions— missions at the direct command of Unomundo.

Morales disregarded the rank of colonel preceding Gunther's name. He knew that rank to be only a political ploy and face-saving gesture to the hundreds of generals, *generalissimos*, and supreme commanders throughout the hemisphere. When Colonel Gunther appeared at the scene of an action, the generals introduced him to their officers as only their liaison to the International. In fact, Gunther commanded all the forces of the International, generals, colonels, privates, mercenaries—every soldier who took the gold or dollars of Unomundo.

That meant Unomundo himself had dispatched Colonel Gunther to command the search and capture of Carl Lyons.

And the orders had said, "Capture At Any Cost."

This would be a major military operation, not the routine day-to-day administration of the International's hundreds of companies. Colonel Gunther would command the irregular group of *desconocidos* who would enter the search area and the uniformed Guatemalan army units surrounding the search area.

As second-in-command to Colonel Gunther, this would be a chance for Morales to repay the generosity of Unomundo—and to distinguish himself.

A chance to gain even greater rank and wealth within the International.

He would capture this *norteamericano*.

At any cost.

11

"¡Señor Stone! *Señor!*"

"Up, specialist!"

Hands shook Lyons. He opened his eyes. Two shadows stood in the predawn blue. The lines of rifles cut their forms. Reflexes caused Lyons to startle. A hand pressed down on his chest, not trying to pin him, not threatening, only firm and reassuring.

A third shadow crouched next to Lyons. He heard Nate's voice calming him. The strong hand gripped Lyons's shoulder. "It's us. Nate and Xagil. Pedro Saquic. We need you to come with us. You up to it, specialist?"

"Yeah, I'm awake." Lyons looked out the picture window at the blue-touched violet of the sky. Perhaps another half hour to dawn. "What's going on?"

"EGP. Remember the Walther 300 Magnum? You called it the space rifle? Here."

Lyons took the Walther 2000 sniping rifle. The bulky untramodern weapon utilized the 'bullpup' configuration. The designers had placed the receiver group and the magazine in the buttstock, behind the grip and trigger housing. The rifle would fire 5.56mm or 7.62mm NATO, but this one was chambered for the

Winchester .300 Magnum, a cartridge of enhanced ballistics, velocity and striking power.

Two years before, Lyons had taken the rifle from a member of an assassination team assigned to murder the president of Guatemala as the first strike in Unomundo's seizure of the nation. He had left it with Nate as a gift.

"Your eyes as good as they were a few years ago?" Nate asked.

Turning the weapon over in his hands, Lyons checked the bipod legs and the plastic caps sealing the 3X-9X ART II scope. The metal smelled recently oiled. "Yeah, what you want me to do with this?"

"Here's the case. Put on your pants and get moving...."

Five minutes later the four men moved through the blue predawn light, following a tire-beaten track through the meadows and forest. Each man put his feet in the footprints of the man ahead. Lyons carried the fiberglass and foam case of the Walther. Around his waist he wore a black nylon web belt and a Colt Government Model—the gear of a years-dead Fascist mercenary.

They came to an east-west ridgeline. Dawn burned behind the pines. Pedro Saquic, a teenager perhaps two years older than Xagil, who was fourteen, led them to a stretch of exposed volcanic stone. Paralleling the ridgeline, they ran along the naked stone, stepping over fractures alive with grass and ferns. Their feet left no marks on the mountainside.

As the first daylight appeared they cut into the forest. Pedro found a foot trail of hard-packed dirt, and they continued to the crest of the ridge. Then Pedro signaled for the men to stop. When Lyons saw the other three men form an outward-facing star, their eyes and rifles covering arc sectors of the forest and dry brush around them, he took his arc. They crouched there, listening, Lyons keeping his hand on the grip of his cocked-and-locked-Colt.

At first Lyons heard only the sounds of the forest. The wings of a bird rushed through the air above him. Something rustled through the ground's matting of leaves. Stirrings of wind swayed the trees above them.

Then in the distance, he heard a tool striking wood. The sound continued, pausing for a moment, then resuming, regular, monotonous. Work. Ahead someone chopped wood.

Pedro moved fast, his patched dark pants and black wool shirt disappearing as Lyons turned. Lyons grabbed the Walther's case and followed the other men down the trail.

The trail zigzagged down a steep mountainside. Last in the line, Lyons heard the others sliding and stumbling as they ran. Within two minutes they came to the woodcutter.

A middle-aged Quichenero with a pain-lined face, the woodcutter talked with the teenage Pedro. They had the same features. Father and son. The woodcutter saw Lyons and set down his ax. Dragging his stiff left leg, the man walked to Lyons with his right hand extended.

"This is Juan Saquic," Nate told Lyons as Juan introduced himself in *Quiche*. "He fought with us that night."

Lyons shook hands and nodded gravely. "Without Juan and all his *compañeros*, we could have done nothing. I hope his leg does not pain him."

Nate translated into *Quiche*.

Juan answered, saying it was nothing.

Behind him, as he continued down the trail, Lyons heard the monotonous chopping resume. Nate lagged behind for a moment to explain. "The sound is the all clear. It's the signal for the other groups to keep coming."

"Where are the Commies?"

"Soon."

Another few switchbacks brought them to a cluster of adobe houses. Chickens and pigs scattered as they approached. A woman in *traje* washed the dishes under a faucet. She smiled to the three men, then dropped the dishes and started upright at the sight of Lyons. She ran into the house.

Lyons heard Nate call out. Two boys, no older than fifteen, waved to Nate from the hillside overlooking the houses. Both boys had old long-barreled 12-gauge shotguns. Then from downhill an old man answered. He had a sawed-off Remington pump shotgun.

"We stop here for a minute. See that faucet? The running water? That's some of the hundred grand."

Lyons asked, pointing at the teenagers, "They the reserve?"

"In case the EG get around us."

"Shotguns against automatic rifles?"

Nate gave him an evil grin. "You see shotguns. You don't see the M-16s and grenades. And here, meet your godson."

"What godson? What're you talking about?"

A woman prodded a toddler toward Lyons. Lyons went down to one knee and extended a hand to shake. He and the child touched hands, the "handshake" leaving a smear of dirt and snot on Lyons's hand. Lyons laughed and the child cried at the noise the blond stranger made.

Then they moved again. Running along another ridgeline, they came to a second woodcutter. The old man wore different *traje*—red stripes on his white peasant pants, different embroidery on his shirt and a different cut to his black wool coat. Apparently they had crossed into the ancestral lands of another pueblo. The woodcutter stopped his work and talked with the men. The woodcutter gave Lyons a few suspicious glances but Nate explained. Finally the old man returned to his work. Nate briefed Lyons.

"Okay, we move slow now. There's others up ahead, waiting. We'll check in with them, then I take you to your position."

Continuing at a quick walk, they stayed on the path. Pedro made a quiet bird-clucking sound in his throat. They approached the crest of another hill. Pedro stopped and made more bird noises.

Someone answered with a low whistle. A man motioned from the brush. He wore patched, black store-bought pants and a camouflage fatigue shirt. Bandoliers of ammunition for his M-16 crisscrossed his chest.

He led them to the crest, where he dropped down flat and crawled. The others followed. Then they saw the killground.

Years before, the slopes had been cleared, but pine stumps remained here and there. Farmers had already begun preparing the fields for the coming rainy season, cutting down the cornstalks and burning them in piles. The morning air smelled of ash piles. The mountainsides had been hoe-turned to expose dark, dusty soil tangled with decaying cornstalks.

To the west, for a thousand yards, the fields sloped down, then up to a steep ridge topped by pines about six hundred yards away. The gentle slopes continued for another six hundred yards to the north, where the cornfields ended against another wall of forest. The converging slopes created a triangular minivalley.

The trail came from the forest and curved through the center of the fields. On both sides nothing would provide cover.

"We've got men in those trees," Nate said, pointing to the pines six hundred yards away. "And we'll be here. When they're within twenty yards of us, we'll hit them. When they run back, our men in the trees will hit them."

"When they're down there," Lyons said, looking at the center of the valley four hundred yards away, "they'll be at the extreme range of your 5.56 rifles."

"That's why you'll be..." Nate pointed to the forest at the north of the small valley, "right there. You hit what we miss."

"I get a spotter?"

"You need one?"

"Guess not." He looked down to where the trail came from the trees. "When do they get here?"

"Soon. A runner came in and said they're a half hour behind him."

"How many?"

"More than ten."

"You want prisoners?"

Nate shook his head.

"How do we know they're Communists? They—"

"No one cares about their politics. They murdered two men. They raped a woman. They die."

"On my way," Lyons said.

Lyons scrambled backward. Twenty yards downhill he ran to the north, staying well below the ridge. The slope continued gradually uphill, and he followed a network of sheeptrails weaving through the grass. As the slope became steep, brush and debris choked the forest floor. He thrashed through, finally coming to another trail. The trail cut to the west. Lyons followed the trail through dense stands of pines. In shadowy clearings stumps and wood chips marked where the woodcutters had worked.

To his left he saw daylight through the trees. He zipped up his black nylon jacket to cover his T-shirt and pale throat, then eased through the shadows, using the Walther's case to push through the branches.

He almost fell off the mountain. Stopping himself as one boot found air, Lyons saw the cornfields beneath him. He eased back and checked his position.

Although he wasn't looking down at the center of the valley, he still had a total field of fire. On his left he saw the line of Nate's squad along the east ridge. Lyons counted seven men. On his right he saw what looked like the forms of men in the deep grass and brush at the forest's edge.

Straight south, almost a mile away, the trail left the forest. The wide, easy footpath cut through the fields, then ran up the slope to where Nate waited.

Taking the sniper rifle and two 6-round magazines from the case, Lyons settled into a prone firing position. He pushed down the bipod legs. He flipped up the plastic scope caps. Pressing his cheek against the polished wood of the stock, he sighted through the ART scope.

If Nate's friends and in-laws had been marksmen this would be a deadly ambush. The only escape for the guerrillas would be to rush into the autoweapon fire of the line of riflemen on the ridge, or to sprint back to the forest. An uphill run into the point-blank fire of seven automatic rifles or a marathon run across open ground to the forest.

Thumbing out the first cartridge of a magazine, he checked the casing for corrosion. The swaged soft-tip bullet and the hand loaded cartridge looked perfect. The discoloration of the brass would not affect the trajectory.

Lyons waited. Around him, as the sun lighted the mountains, birds broke the silence with their territorial songs. He heard wings rustling through branches. He listened for wind. But nothing moved. Only the birds. In the distance he heard an ax cutting wood.

He took a scrap of paper from his coat pocket—an unused Guatemalan customs form. Tearing the heavy paper in half, then chewing the paper like gum, he made two earplugs.

A point of red appeared in the distant tree line, and Lyons saw white pants and a red shirt emerge from the forest. Lyons zoomed the ART scope onto the chest of the Quichero, a teenager with blood on his shirt. He noted the setting on the scope. That would be his extreme range.

As the next minutes passed a line of forms came from the forest. An *indígena* in white peasant pants and a red shirt led them, his hands behind his back. The first man behind the *indígena* held a rope that went to the *indígena's* neck, like a leash. Lyons counted fifteen men—he assumed them to be men, as he saw no long hair in the line. The fifteen wore a collection of dark clothing and camouflage. They all carried weapons. Lyons saw only small packs on their backs.

Using the camouflaged chest of a guerrilla wearing sunglasses, Lyons set the scope at midrange in the valley, four hundred yards.

Only two steps separated the *indígena* from the first guerrilla holding the rope. Lyons watched the grassy ridge where Nate waited. One of the prone forms slipped downhill, then snaked to the far end of the line of riflemen. The two prone forms met for a moment, then the moving form went from man to man. Lyons hoped that Nate had worked out a way to avoid killing or wounding the prisoner.

Pulling back the actuator, then clicking down the safety, Lyons finally gripped the Walther. He sighted on the last man in the line. Against the turned earth of the fields, the horizontal light of the rising sun lighted the man like a sign.

Lyons watched as the line of guerrillas filed up the last switchback. He watched the scene with his left eye as he kept his cheek against the Walther, his right eye on line with the scope.

At the head of the line, the *indígena* started. Lyons saw the man with the rope jerk and spin. The *indígena* fell. Simultaneously, dust puffed along the line of guerrillas, their arms flying out, men staggering, several falling.

Sighting a step ahead of a running man, Lyons squeezed off the first shot. The trigger had a perfect smooth pull. The heavy rifle absorbed most of the recoil. Lyons returned the reticle to the running man. Lyons followed him, then he saw the man's back as he ran away and Lyons squeezed off one careful shot. The guerrilla dropped.

Now the sound of rifles came to Lyons, the ripping autobursts and individual shots echoing in the small valley. Muted by the paper wads in his ears, the ambush sounded as distant as a memory.

Again, keeping his right eye in line with the scope, he scanned the scene. At this distance he could hear no voices, only shooting, but he knew the guerrillas below him screamed and moaned and shouted to one another as they died. He had executed point-blank ambushes. He knew the sounds of panic and death.

He watched a guerrilla rush the ridgeline, firing his submachine gun in a desperate attempt to suppress the unseen riflemen for the second—the impossibly long moment—the guerrilla needed to break through the ambush and out to survival. His pack exploded in a ball of flame as through-and-through rifle slugs detonated a device he carried.

Other guerrillas sprawled on the trail and used their comrades' bodies for cover. Long-distance rifle fire came down into their backs. Two guerrillas realized they lay in crossfire and sprinted downhill.

Lyons sighted on the slower man. Leading him a step, Lyons touched the trigger three times. As the muzzle flashed the third time, Lyons saw his target already falling. He found the last man with the ART optics.

Weaving, zigzagging, never stopping as he raced erratically through the turned earth of the cornfields, the guerrilla had succeeded in avoiding the fire of both lines of riflemen. Lyons added his marksmanship to the game.

Always keeping the reticle line one step ahead of the dodging form, Lyons sent 220-grain slugs into the man's desperate pattern of evasion.

The guerrilla fell.

Scanning the dark turned earth of the fields, Lyons saw nothing moving. Then the red-shirted *indígena* scrambled over the ridge. One of the Quichenero riflemen pulled him into the grass. The firing continued.

Single aimed shots popped. Dust puffed around the sprawled forms as the two groups of riflemen zeroed their fire.

Lyons watched the scene, the Walther ready, as the firing died away and the Quichenero militiamen emerged from cover. They fired into every corpse before finally confirming the kills with machetes.

Then Lyons returned the rifle to its case.

12

Alfredo contemplated Cheryl Tiegs. The poster of the blond beauty hung on the wall at the foot of his bed, where he could gaze upon her night and day, her smile and her long tanned legs transporting him from his miserable duty in the altiplano, from the garrison in Azatlan.

Looking at her, he forced himself not to hear the voices of his soldiers outside. He refused to hear their stupid jokes and laughter. He forgot their pranks. He thought of beaches, of surfing, of suntan oil....

Did Cheryl surf? Perhaps if he went to California, he would see her at the beach, riding the waves, her blond hair whipping in the wind. He would wait until she left the ocean and then...then what?

He could not demand to see her identification and then make talk like he did with the tourist girls. The tourist girls always trembled a little when they handed him their papers. He always studied the documents very closely. He let the tourist girls stand there and think of all the newspapers and books from Amnesty International. The bad, bad army. Evil! Terrorizing students, shooting *indígenas*, killing babies with bayonets—just like the U.S. Cavalry in the Old West, making America safe for McDonald's drive-ins and Sassoon and Walt Disney.

In California he would not be a lieutenant with the responsibility for maintaining order and fighting the Communists. In California the Communists made movies and drove Rolls Royces. Anyway, he would not wear his uniform at the beach. He had good muscles and a better tan than any California Communist. Perhaps he would wear his black beret.

Perhaps he should get reassignment to the coast. There, he could practice surfing. When he went to California he could surf with everyone. And he should practice his English. On the coast, he could talk English with the other surfers.

"Hang ten!" he said out loud. He wished the blond *norteamericano*, the one with the bag of contraband, had brought surf music. Surf music would make Alfredo a better surfer. So he could meet Cheryl and make out with her on the beach.

Shouts broke into his daydreams. He heard shouted commands. The sergeant. Prancing about with his stomach stuck out, pretending to be a big soldier.

Sergeant Guerrero, who wanted to be military commander of Azatlan. What an honor, what a responsibility.

The lieutenant contemplated his responsibility. To defend Azatlan from the Communist hordes. What would he do if ten thousand EGP attacked little Azatlan, trampling the cornfields with their Nicaraguan boots, scaring the *indígenas*, shooting their Russian rifles at the brave soldiers defending beautiful little Azatlan?

What would the lieutenant do? In the university he had studied history. For the answer to his dilemma he mentally leafed through the pages of European warfare, the battles, the brilliant campaigns, the victories.

And history gave him the answer! If confronted by overwhelming numbers of enemies, if confronted by certain defeat, do as the French and surrender! Do as the English and retreat!

Wait for the U.S. Marines! The marines would know how to surf. They learned to surf at their base in California. They could teach him.

First, shoot down the Communists, then surf. Just like in the movies.

Wood splintering, the door to his room flew open. Alfredo started, turning in the bed as soldiers rushed at him. Hands pinned him down.

"Get away from me, you stupid—"

A fist smashed into his face. Then pain exploded in his gut as a steel rifle butt slammed down. Fists came down in a fury of shocks and he felt himself dragged from his bed, his bare feet dragging over the concrete of the floor. Brilliant morning sunlight blinded him.

Kicks came as his body, now a mass of pains and nausea, flew through the air and flopped over the planks of a truck. He wore only underwear, and the rough planks jammed splinters into his hands and knees. He saw soldiers climb into the troop truck and then the boots came at him and light flashed in his skull, the shock of a kick rolling him back.

The truck lurched into motion. Gears clanked, the planks creaked and swayed as the wheels bumped over the ruts. His captors shouted questions into his face as the truck left the compound and accelerated over the cobblestones of the village street.

"Who was the *norteamericano*?"

"Why have you not reported that criminal?"

Alfredo opened his mouth to speak. A hand grabbed his ear and slammed his head sideways into the planks.

"They talked with you! What did they say?"

Finally he screamed out his own question. "Who?"

A boot drove into his gut. Obscenities and fists came down at him. He curled against the wood side of the troop transport, trying to protect his face with his arms. Boots found his kidneys and spine, arching him backward.

They would kill him. Kick him and beat him to death. He knew it. Floating in a half light of pain, he accepted the sentence of death. No more thought of who, no more thought of struggle, no more thought of escape from pain—no more thought. Wait for the end.

And he thought he had died. No more pain came. No fists, no boots. No shouted questions.

But he still lived. He felt the truck speeding over the road, the wheels jumping on the rutted road.

Opening an eye, he saw dust swirling behind the truck. He saw the cornfields going to the edge of Azatlan, the whitewashed walls and roofs seeming to rise directly from the fields. Clouding dust paled the image.

Voices. Around him men shouted over the noise of the truck to talk. He listened but he could not understand. Truck noise and the slamming of his blood—his pain, his fear—beat in his ears.

Fear and hope returned. He rode without moving. He wanted them to think he had passed out. He wanted them to think he had died. He did not want the fists and boots and questions again.

The truck labored uphill. Alfredo felt the gears shift. Azatlan appeared for a moment as the truck followed a curve, then the white cluster of houses and roofs receded into the distance, disappearing into the yellow dust.

After an eternity he felt the truck slowing.

Hands took him, jerking him to his feet. He saw camouflage and black berets. Soldiers. He could not see insignia. Army units on active duty. If the soldiers had been paramilitary police, they would wear armbands.

They dragged him to the end of the truck and shoved him. Crying out in panic, he raised his hands as he hit the road, his arm snapping and his face smashing into the dust.

They laughed as they grabbed him, pain making him scream and plead, the words coming incoherently as they dragged him across the road. Every movement made his wrist flop. And every flop made him cry out with pain.

Trucks were parked everywhere, and soldiers stood around in groups watching as the two men dragged him to their officer. With only a red beret identifying him as a field commander, the officer leaned against a radio jeep, waiting.

They stood him in front of the officer, holding his arms, keeping him upright. Alfredo saw his reflection in the officer's sunglasses. Then, in the moment before the officer spoke, he saw the silver insignia flashing from the beret:

The stylized, brutal-looking eagle and the twin lightning strikes.

No unit of the army of Guatemala used that eagle for identification.

"Where are the gringos?" The officer spoke in a cold, quiet voice.

"What...what ones?"

Smiling, the officer reached out and lightly backhanded Alfredo's broken wrist, again and again.

The soldiers held him as he arched backward, trying to escape the pain.

"Answer."

Alfredo gasped out words. "Gringos come. Hippies, girls, tourists, collectors—"

"Where is the one who wears the clothes of *indígenas*?"

They meant the *norteamericano* known as Nate. Who had married a Quichenera. Tell them fast, stop the pain. "He lives in the mountains with his wife, he—"

"Where?"

"He has a house. I have never been there. He comes into town—"

"And the other one?"

"Stone. He came days ago. He walked to the town. He went with Nate."

"Where?"

"I don't know. To the mountains. To his house."

The colonel grabbed his arm and twisted...the world became a place of darkness and crashing pain.

Alfredo lay in the dirt. The colonel looked down at him, the sunglasses mirroring Alfredo's bloody face. Alfredo saw the trademark on the sunglasses. Porsche-Carrera, the sunglasses of a rich man, like the ones they wore in California.

"Tell me where and you live."

But Alfredo did not know.

13

Searching the fields, Quicheneros gathered the weapons of the dead guerrillas, stripping off packs and bandoliers. A group of boys hurried back and forth from the old woodcutters on the other side of the ridge, dragging back cordwood and branches. The boys laughed and called out to one another as they stacked the wood in the midst of the bodies. A man directed them to crisscross the wood, to form a pyre. The Quicheneros would burn the corpses.

Walking across the slope, Lyons paced through the slaughter, conducting his own search, not for weapons and ammunition but for identification. He stopped to examine one body. The Quicheneros had already stripped off the man's jacket and pack. Two bullets had killed the man almost instantly with through-and-through heart wounds. Other bullets had shattered the legs, another burst had torn away most of the head. Flies had already found the wounds and puddled blood.

The dead man wore almost-new boots. The polyester pants had dirt on the knees and a washed-out oil stain on the seat. But the washings had not yet erased the permanent-press creases. Lyons found nothing in the pockets.

Lyons went on to the next corpse, the guerrilla who had the training—or courage—to try to break out of the ambush by rushing the line of riflemen.

The guerrilla lay on his face in the dirt, his back charred a dusky black by the explosion of flame. Someone had severed his head with a machete. Lyons squatted next to the corpse and looked into the ashes, blackened metal and glistening flesh of the dead man's back. The iridescent-green forms of flies swarmed on the exposed bones and flesh.

Lyons could not positively identify the device that had burned the guerrilla, but the ashes stank of petroleum and plastic. The impacts of slugs punching through the man's chest had sprayed flaming plastic over the dirt and rotting cornstalks before the dying man fell. The fire had left scabs of black sticky residue on the ground.

Perhaps a workshop-made incendiary bomb.

Examining the body more closely, Lyons lifted one of the hands.

No calluses. The guerrilla had not been a farmer or a worker. The nails showed recent clipping. Lyons saw clean cuticles and only superficial dirt on the palms— not the encrusted, deeply ingrained filth of difficult and uncertain survival in a mountain wilderness, on the run from security forces that watched every town, not every place offering soap and water.

Next, Lyons checked the man's pockets, finding car keys and the keys to a house or apartment.

Quickly Lyons slap-checked the other pockets and took out a Swiss army knife and a disposable cigarette lighter. No identification. No money or credit cards. No cigarettes. All of that could have been in the small backpack. Or perhaps the man had left his personal belongings in his car.

"Daytripper..." Lyons muttered.

Finally standing, waving the swirling flies away from his face, Lyons looked for Nate. He saw the marine-gone-Quichenero on the ridge, inventorying weapons and ammunition. Lyons jogged up the hill to him.

Galil rifles stood in threes, and munitions had been spread out on a plastic tarp taken from a guerrilla pack. The collection included several types of hand-thrown grenades, a few rifle grenades, bandoliers, pistols, even claymore mines with det-cord and electric firing systems.

"You question the kid yet?" Lyons looked over the teenager the guerrillas had forced to guide them through the mountains.

"Wait. I will. He's still shaking."

"When you do, ask him if any of the guerrillas drove a Mustang."

"¿Que?" Nate looked at Lyons with disbelief. "What? What are you talking about?"

Lyons passed the keys to Nate. As the other man examined the ring of keys, Lyons explained, "One key goes to the ignition of a Ford Mustang. Got them out of one of—" he pointed to the burned man—"that one's pockets. No ID saying where he's from, but he isn't from out here. His clothes are almost clean, his shoes are new, and I bet he had a hot shower yesterday morning."

Speaking quickly to the boy, Nate started toward the corpses. Lyons followed, calling out, "The guerrillas usually this well equipped?"

"I'm not sure they were guerrillas but..." Nate did not complete his answer. He stopped at the burned man. "This one?"

With his boot Nate rolled the severed head face up. The face showed a day's stubble.

"Look at his shoes," Lyons pointed. "His clothes. His hands. They find any identification in the packs?"

"No. Only weapons and food."

Lyons watched as Nate examined the dead man. He prodded the pectoral muscles, then jerked up a blackened pants leg to see the precisely laced boots and thick calf muscles. Nate confirmed Lyon's suspicions.

"Provocador del Ejército—a Provocateur. And not the army of the poor. There are bastards in the government who go out and claim to be guerrillas. If people help them, say anything, *los provocadores* kill them as an example. A warning to the pueblos." Nate kicked the dead man's head down the mountainside. "He was a whore for the Nazis...."

"What? Unomundo?" Lyons asked.

"Unomundo is only one of them. There are many. Many more."

For the next half hour Nate and Lyons searched the other bodies. They went quickly from corpse to corpse, and when they had finished with their examinations, Quicheneros dragged the dead men off to the pile of wood.

Nate and Lyons confirmed that the strangers had not slept in the mountains more than one night: they wore clean clothes and their packs contained only munitions and food in cans and bottles. Some of the other dead men also had keys in their pockets. The search also confirmed from where the men had come—one had his food wrapped in a plastic supermarket bag from the capital.

"They bought the food in Guatemala City."

Nate nodded.

Then they found a fly-swarming corpse that revealed a connection from beyond Guatemala. Though the man had dark hair and brown skin like a *mestizo*, he had not been born in Central America.

"Hijo de puta!" Nate cursed, squatting next to the dead man, looking down at his Southeast Asian features.

The machetes of the Quicheneros had opened the throat and chest of the corpse. The chin of the guerrilla had been severed by a machete hack. Nate found the hunk of jaw in the dirt and fitted it onto the gaping wound to reconstruct the face. He waved away the flies and pointed:

"This one is a gook! A Viet!"

"You positive?"

Nate dismissed the question with a low, guttural expression in *Quiche*, then he completed his answer with a demonstration. The ex-marine shifted in his squat. He had squatted with his weight balanced on the balls of his feet, his elbows resting on his knees, his hands crossed in front of him—in the manner of a Quichenero. As Lyons watched, Nate eased his center of gravity backward, his boot soles going flat on the earth, the position of his arms changing until his knees pressed his armpits—like a Vietnamese.

"What do you want? I was there two years. If that *puto*—" he spat on the mangled face of the dead Vietnamese "—was still alive, I could talk to him. And you ask me if I'm sure. You from Washington, D.C.?

Why don't you think I can know something? I got to wear a suit and a tie and carry a briefcase to know?''

"What I mean," Lyons elaborated on his question, "are there any Vietnamese living in Guatemala?"

Shaking his head, Nate went through the pockets of the dead man. Though blood saturated the denim jacket and pants, creating slabs of gore, Nate reached into every pocket. He found a wad of folded papers. He wiped his hands and the papers on the dead man's clean pants before unfolding the sheets.

Nate showed him a page with the letterhead of a hotel in Tegucigalpa.

Now Lyons agreed with Nate. "A foreigner."

"Who stays in first class hotels."

"The agency?"

"Maybe."

The papers had columns of Spanish expressions—questions and simple answers—matched with columns of translations, some in Vietnamese, others in English. Ball-point-pen scribbles of accent marks and phonetics had been added on some of the Spanish words. The dead man had been studying Spanish phrases.

"In from Honduras, but didn't speak Spanish," Nate wondered out loud.

"The agency would teach their specialists Spanish...."

"Didn't teach you," Nate countered.

"Then maybe he's a mercenary? What do you think?"

Without answering, Nate smoothed one slip of paper. He held it up for Lyons.

The foreigner had known another language. In a ball-point-pen scrawl matching the handwriting of the other sheets, he had scribbled a note. But Nate and Lyons could only read the numbers, because the Vietnamese had written in the Cyrillic alphabet of the Soviet Union.

Finally Lyons spoke. "You've got to talk to that kid."

Gathering all the papers, they returned to the ridge where Nate quietly questioned the now-free teenage prisioner in *Quiche* and broken Spanish. Lyons heard the words, *"guerrillos... putos... castellaño... norteamericano...."*

Though he could not understand most of the talk, Lyons listened and observed. He had questioned thousands of suspects and witnesses in his years as a policeman and then later as a detective. His partners in Able Team joked that he had no interrogation techniques other than shouted demands and sudden pain. Lyons called that "expedient interrogation," not questioning. In combat or hot pursuit he needed answers quickly. He got answers.

But Lyons knew the technique of questioning. And now he watched Nate questioning the teenager. He heard Nate repeating and rephrasing questions, perhaps trying for details the boy had skipped over. He saw Nate smile and frown and gesture. When the boy looked at Lyons instead of considering a question, Nate regained his attention with a friendly touch, then repeated the question without impatience or irritation or anger. He coaxed the boy to remember.

Finally Nate turned to Lyons. "Got the answer. They wanted the *norteamericano* living in the mountains. Me."

14

In the smoky warmth of the living room Lyons and Nate spread out the captured documents on the rough-hewn table. They talked until Marylena brought her husband and his guest lunch. Though the young Quichenera spoke very little Spanish and no English, the two men went quiet as she served them. In addition to a skinny chicken she spooned out beans, steamed corn and chili, served with tortillas. Then a side dish appeared.

"What's this?" Lyons asked.

Nate discussed the question with his wife. "*Cerviche*."

"How could it be *cerviche*? You're hours from the ocean."

"Loot. There was tuna fish in their packs."

With the red pepper and spices, the tuna fish became—"Interesting," Lyons commented, nodding his approval to Marylena. "Tuna fish with *salsa*. Try it."

Nate slapped some of the *cerviche* on a tortilla. He ate it but did not take another serving. He nodded approval to his wife, but said, "Still tuna fish. None of this for years."

"They don't sell cans of it up here?"

"Makes Guatemalans sick. Too much protein. Stomach can't take it. You eat it. Too hot?"

Lyons laughed. He spooned the blood-red preparation onto a tortilla. "After Sri Lanka nothing's too hot. They make salads out of jalapeños there. They got a tiny little pepper about the size of a .22 bullet that is so hot, it goes through your guts just as fast as a bullet, except it hurts more."

"Hot."

"Makes for napalm shits."

"Like that one with the bombs in his pack?"

"Not that hot." Lyons had given the purpose of the improvised incendiary thought. "They had grenades. Shrapnel and CN. They had claymores. Then those firebombs. Special purpose. They had something in mind."

"I know what they wanted."

"They intended to hit a house. Even a grenade or a claymore won't do the job on an adobe house. Not like an incendiary bomb. Not like CN gas. They were out here to either assassinate someone in an ugly, ugly way—"

"Me. Make an example. Because I fought Unomundo."

"Or they'd use the CN and the firebomb to get you out of your house, alive."

"Interrogate?"

"About us. They don't want you. They want who paid you that hundred thousand. Which means we got to get you and your family out."

"To where? Across the border into Mexico?"

Lyons shook his head. "The International owns battalions of the Mexican army, at least they did at one time. That could all be over; I don't know for sure, but I don't want to chance it. We'll have to go all the way north. Even if the International's got paid-for politicians in Washington, they don't run the country.''

''I can't get any money out. There's no way—''

''A flight north, all expenses paid. You were in on a Team operation. And now the bad guys are looking to take you. That makes you a definite security risk. That makes you qualified for Team assistance. Is there an airfield around here that we could use?''

''For an agency plane? Maybe they want that. Wait for you to call. They fly in with a kill squad.''

''We've got pilots I trust. We'll fly you out, keep you safe until we can resolve the problem.''

Nate went to the long picture window overlooking the valley of Azatlan. ''And what about the people here? My in-laws, my neighbors? Who takes care of them?''

''Your wife's sister goes with you. They don't want your neighbors. But judging by what I saw today, if they send out some goons, your neighbors can deal with death squads.''

''Yeah, and what if they bring in another thousand soldiers and search for me house by house?''

''Unless they get the Guatemalan army, where will they get the soldiers? We burned the last thousand they hired. It would take them months to put another mercenary army together. And in that time, we'll hit Unomundo again.''

Staring out the window, Nate said nothing for a minute. Then he cursed, ''The shit never stops!''

''And it won't stop until we do that Nazi. Do him in.''

"There it is. All right. We'll take my family north, but then we go hunting. I'm not going to hide in some house, waiting for the death squad. Understand?"

"I understand, exactly."

Leaning forward, Nate peered intently out the window. He studied something in the distance, then turned away and rushed to a shelf. He came back with a pair of OD binoculars. Again he stared into the distance.

"What's going on?" Lyons asked.

"Army trucks. I see five. That's almost a company of soldiers. Major movement."

Lyons scanned the sky. "No helicopters."

Nate gave him the binoculars. "Watch. I'll send Xagil out to—"

"No, don't. If we have to move, we don't want to leave him behind. If this is bad news, won't someone bring you word?"

Considering that for a moment, Nate nodded.

"Time to pack up. We can't risk going that way—" Lyons looked to the town. "Any other way out to a major town? I'll need to make a call to the U.S."

"The roads will wreck the truck. The cooperative needs to have a truck—"

"Leave the pickup. Can your wife and her sister walk as far as the highway? If the army's got five truckloads of soldiers down there, they'll have men anywhere their troop trucks can go."

"We can walk to Aguacatan, then go on to Huehuetenango. One or two days..." Nate surveyed the interior of his house, the handmade furniture, the rough plastered walls, the long picture window. "I know they will break that window...."

"More than that. When they find you aren't here, they'll waste the place."

Nate stepped across the room to the plaster and adobe wall. He laughed and gave the wall a slap. "There's more dirt where this came from. Built it before. Can build it again."

15

Cornstalks and dust exploded from the field as the gleaming blue-and-white executive helicopter descended to the hilltop. Soldiers turned away from the rotor storm, holding their berets and squinting against the blowing dust. As if saluting, Lieutenant-Colonel Ortega shielded his sunglasses from the wind-thrown pebbles. The pilot cut the engine power. Colonel Ortega watched the rotors slowing, waiting at the radio jeep while his soldiers rushed into the swirling dust to open the helicopter's side door. Two men stepped out, one a Guatemalan and the other a hulking foreigner with whitish-blond hair—the man rumored to be Colonel Gunther. Colonel Ortega waited at the jeep as the two men crossed the field.

The overweight Guatemalan—his tailored suit perfect, his chest puffed out, his jowls like bladders above his tight collar—snapped salutes to all the soldiers. Surprised, the soldiers only stared.

But the foreigner did not waste time or motion on pompous pseudomilitarism. His mirrored sunglasses scanned the scene, counting the trucks and soldiers, checking their equipment and appearance, pausing for a moment on the distant town, then fixing on Colonel Ortega himself. Despite his decision not to respect the hireling Guatemalan and the foreign liaison officer, Ortega felt his back go straight, his shoulders squaring. He stood at full height, in parade-correct posture, to receive the strangers.

"I am Colonel Morales, retired. And I present Colonel Gunther, who will be our liaison to the International."

Colonel Ortega did not return the salute of the fat ex-colonel. Nor did he extend his hand for a handshake. But he did watch the towering Gunther.

"That is the village?" Gunther asked, pointing to Azatlan.

"Yes."

"And that road?" His arm traced the line of the dirt track leading into the mountains. "My map showed that it went no further than the second ridge. Is that correct?"

Ortega nodded. "The International improved the road as far as the burned-out cave—you know what I speak of?"

"The disaster!" Colonel Morales shook his head at the thought of the destruction of Unomundo's mercenary army.

The lieutenant-colonel continued, his lips curling into a sneer. "Where the gringos and *indígenas* wiped out the foreigners. Past there, the road continues. But you must know the place, correct?"

"No—" Gunther countered.

"I had been betrayed and taken prisoner in the capital. I could not defend our leader in his time of—"

"That is history!" Gunther talked over the ex-colonel. "And it need not be described or explained.

We now have the opportunity to take two of the *nor-teamericanos* responsible for that defeat and question them. That is the objective. My map shows that the road ends there. But you say the road continues. To where?''

Lieutenant Ortega motioned across the road to where three platoon leaders studied an over-sized map. Printed from satellite information received from NASA, the computer-generated loops and shadings of the topography detailed every town, road and trail in the region.

Though the foreigner stood six-foot-seven, he seemed to glide across the earth, the strength of his body compensating for his size. Ortega noticed that Gunther did not wear black leather Oxfords with his suit. Instead he wore black nylon shoes that satisfied the conservative look of his corporate style, yet pro-vided flexibility. The thin neoprene soles did not add to this height. Ortega found himself thinking of the thin-soled slippers of his kung-fu training.

When Gunther traced the lines of the map, his hand confirmed the speculation of Ortega. The enlarged, callused knuckles indicated years of continuous kar-ate training. The deep lines of scars indicated actual combat. No one received scars like those in training. Only in cruel, no-quarter fighting. Striking an enemy in the face might stun or kill, but shattering teeth often gouged the hand of the victor. This foreigner had fought hand-to-hand. Many times. And won.

''Colonel Morales sent a special unit in from this direction.'' The foreigner pointed to where a dirt track wove through the mountains, then indicated the probable line of march through the maze of valleys and ridges. "Our information is that the *norteameri-cano* who associates with the *indígenas* lives in this area—" The blunt, scarred finger drew a circle in the mountains west of the valley road. "He will either fight the special unit or attempt to evade it. He can move most quickly on this road. To the south is the town. To the north a road leads to Huehuetenango. Am I correct? Did you post units to cover that road?"

Ortega nodded. "Certainly. One hundred men now move north from the town, searching every house. A squad of men wait in ambush on this ridgeline, here—" He pointed to a north-south trail running above the valley. "And three squads of men cover the road to the north, the principle foot trail and the area where the dirt road joins the other road. The special unit is on the trail to the west. Colonel Kline's unit covers the eastern region. The gringos cannot move by car or foot without walking into a trap."

"Very good...." Gunther surveyed the valley. "And what did the Lieutenant tell you?"

"What? The one that socialized—"

"With the *norteamericanos*."

"Nothing. He said nothing. He socialized with tourists for companionship. His men tell me he was bored with his duties."

The mirrored sunglasses turned on him. "Is that his blood on you?"

"Ah, yes."

"Will he be available for further interrogation?"

"I shot him."

"No matter...." The blond man looked again at the valley, then to the blue-and-white helicopter. "May I offer the service of the corporation helicopter?"

"Certainly—"

"Yes, yes. My helicopter. One more service to our leader," ex-Colonel Morales sputtered. "However I had placed a request for army aircraft—"

Again the foreigner talked over the middle-aged martinet. "You see, I know one of these *norteamericanos* personally. And I have come four thousand miles with the hope to personally make his capture."

16

Maintaining an even walking pace, the line of men and women snaked along the trail. Pines screened the afternoon sun, allowing only an occasional brilliant shaft of light to penetrate.

Ferns and tangled pine branches touched Lyons's shoulders and scratched across his pack as he walked. Sometimes branches caught in the steel tubing stock of the Galil autorifle he carried.

Lyons walked far behind Nate and the Quichenero pointmen. Despite their numbers, they moved quietly. The wind-rush through the pines hid the soft sounds of their footsteps and the occasional clink of equipment against a weapon.

Behind him Lyons heard the baby cry. He looked back and saw Marylena jostle her baby for a moment, cooing over her shoulder to Quetzal. The baby girl rode in a sling of heavy cloth knotted over Marylena's shoulder, the cloth sling the traditional transportation for Mayan infants. In the intermittent moments of sunlight, the brilliant red of Marylena's *huipile* and the *tzute*—a sling—holding the baby flashed like neon against the forest.

After a rushed departure from the cliff house, Nate led his family north. No one looked back. The two

women carried the family's most precious things—
Marylena carried the baby girl and Marylena's sister
Juana carried three-year old Tecun in a cloth sling.
Lyons carried a rifle and ammunition. In his pack he
carried only food and water for the two-day hike.
Xagil carried a backpack with blankets for the night.

When they came to clusters of houses along the
trail, Nate told the families of his decision to leave for
the United States. His friends in the militia took their
autorifles and walked with him. Teenagers ran ahead
to spread the word to the other families. Lyons cau-
tioned him, but Nate answered, "I want everyone to
know. They'll guard my house. They'll take my
chickens and sheep and take care of them. And if
there's an informer, the Fascists will know I'm gone."

"Straightforward," Lyons agreed. "Hadn't thought
of it like that. Can they go with us as far as the road?"

Nate shook his head. "That is Aguacateca. A different pueblo, different militia, different language.
When we are there, Marylena and Juana and Xagil
must take off their *traje* and wear ladino clothes.
Clothes like you wear, like this." Nate pointed to the
polyester pants and nylon jacket he wore. "So that no
one will know where we are from."

"And our rifles?"

"I brought plastic. We'll cover the rifles to look like
packages. When we get to the road, we bury them.
After that we're only travelers."

But another day of walking remained until they
reached the road. Lyons kept his mind on his
surroundings, his sight and hearing searching for hidden threats or the unusual.

The unusual, he thought, almost laughing. Here I am, in the tropics, hiking in a pine forest that looks like the High Sierras, at almost ten thousand feet in January, and it's like summer. Maybe going into a firefight with men I don't know and can't talk to, and there's women behind me with babies. And they're wearing bright red and blue and purple clothes.

What's unusual is me. Carl Lyons, specialist in the unusual.

Warning Nate not to tell his friends where he's going and why. I've been a secret agent too long, forget what it's like to live in a community, to have friends and family. And responsibilities. Nate may be living in the Departamento de Quiche and talking like a Mayan, but his life is normal.

Once when the line passed through a clearing, Lyons saw the line of Quicheneros who had volunteered to walk with Nate. Young men, old men, teenagers. All carried rifles or shotguns. What a lucky man, Lyons thought. To have that many friends who would risk their lives.

Lyons had only two friends like that. Nate had many. Lyons wondered what role the Mayan culture played in the friendships. Americans always talked about friendship...they made promises and then forgot. Or they hustled the wives of their friends. Or they exploited friendships to get easy jobs. But what did he know about Nate and his friends? Maybe they had their own Peyton Place stories....

But then, Lyons knew that when the community faced the threat of Unomundo, all the men had fought together. In the United States, neighbors couldn't agree on how to quiet barking dogs. And the money.

That had surprised Lyons. Able Team had paid Nate the hundred thousand dollars. And Nate had then set up a cooperative for the community.

Maybe men like Nate—even in the United States—had friends they could depend upon. Maybe culture and hardship had nothing to do with it. Maybe men made their own culture despite the hardships they faced. Or because of the hardships.

Lyons turned the ideas over in his mind as the line continued through the mountains.

After hours of walking they stopped on a fire-scorched ridgeline. Here, the wind howled past them, whistling through the black branches of dead pines. The men gathered around Nate, shaking his hand, talking with him in *Quiche* and broken Spanish. One man shook Lyons's hand and managed to say "Goodbye."

Marylena and Juana tended the children. Xagil unrolled a blanket over the bristly grass and Marylena laid the baby down.

For a minute Lyons stood aside and only watched the farewells. Beyond the group of men and the two women, mountains extended into the distance. White banks of clouds hid mountainsides as the wind drove clouds from the north. Each gust of wind covered the voices of the men and the crooning voices of the women, the wind shrieking through the dead branches, whipping the dry grass, the millions of stalks clicking and squeaking.

Then the Quicheneros left, returning to their families, leaving Lyons and Nate and his family alone on the windswept ridge.

"Now we go alone," Nate told Lyons. He jerked black plastic sacks from his back. "Here."

They wrapped their rifles with the sacks. Rebuckling their bandoliers, they covered the web gear with their jackets. A pistol went into the knitted bag Nate carried.

"About the *traje*?" Lyons glanced to the brilliant-red clothing of the women.

"Tomorrow. It is not that unusual to see women walking to the highway."

Then they heard the rotor throb.

17

With binoculars Gunther studied the forests and mountains. He swept the optics along the mountainsides, searching for trails. He spotted a trail, then a cluster of *indígena* shacks. Checking the map, he penciled down the approximate position of the settlement. Trails led from the settlement to patchworks of fields on the steep mountainsides.

Colonel Morales rode in the co-pilot's seat. He used a second set of binoculars. At his side leaned a Galil automatic rifle.

Indígenas scattered as the helicopter approached. Laughing, the pilot swept low over the fields. Farmers dropped hoes and ran to the cover of the trees. Banking hard, the pilot brought the helicopter over another village. Gunther looked down to see faces flash up, mouths open with fear. Then the people disappeared behind them. Fields appeared.

One man did not run. Leaning on his hoe, his white cotton shirt and white pants sweat-stuck to his body, he stood in his field watching the antics of the helicopter. The pilot called out to Colonel Morales, then pointed at the farmer.

Dropping low, the pilot took the helicopter into a mock combat run, as if he meant to strafe the farmer.

The pilot and Morales laughed as the helicopter swept into an easy arc across the open area. Morales held up his fists and made popping sounds as if he fired a double-grip machine gun.

Gunther watched the man run toward the trees. He looked ahead of the running man. A single pine stood in the fields. Years of trimming for firewood had left the tree arrow straight for the first ten yards. Then the branches spread out. With the low sun behind it, the form of the tree blended into the tree line.

The farmer ran for the tree.

Slapping the back of the pilot's head, Gunther shouted. "Stop your games! You want to kill us?"

Finally seeing the pine, the pilot threw the helicopter into a hard bank. They flashed over the forest, then the mountain dropped away. Gunther looked back at the ridge behind them.

"There was no danger!" The pilot shouted. "I was aware of it."

"And he was, also. That man knew how to destroy a helicopter. Using the pilot as a weapon. He did exactly as I would have. Remember that, the next time you want to play games with Indians."

Subdued, his antics over, the pilot returned to the search. He paralleled the ridgeline of the mountain. Both Gunther and Morales kept their binoculars on the forest. But the pilot spotted the women.

"There! Ahead of us."

The pilot pointed to a naked ridge. Sometime in the past dry season a fire had swept up the mountainside, leaving only blackened, skeletal pines. A few touches of green had appeared in the ashes, but regrowth would not start until the rains in the summer.

Against the ashes and exposed khaki soil of the ridgeline, the red *huipiles* worn by the women seemed to flash like neon. As his passengers found the women with the binoculars, the pilot banked the helicopter through a wide circle.

The women watched the helicopter. Shading their eyes with their hands, they squinted into the sun, watching the strangers watch them.

"Women and babies," Morales commented. "No one else."

"Would two women be alone there?" Gunther kept his binoculars on the mountaintop, searching the fallen trees and shadows for any other detail. "There are no sheep. I don't see any baskets. Why would they be there?" Gunther noted the position on the topographical map. "And that trail comes from our area of search...."

Gunther saw that the trail zigzagged north through the mountains and finally ended at the east-west road between Nebaj and Huehuetenango. Platoon one watched the zigzagging foot trail. Platoon two waited where the trail met the Huehue-Nebaj road. A few miles to the east, platoon three watched the road winding north.

"My Colonel," the pilot called back. "We have only a few more minutes of fuel. Should I radio for the crew to stand by for another refuelling? Or can we refuel in the morning?"

"They can refuel during the night. We will be leaving at first light. Radio the commander. Tell platoon one, the ambush unit on the trail, to remain on one hundred percent alert through the night. Repeat, one hundred percent. All night.

"And one more time. I want the blond man alive. Tell the commander to tell the soldiers again and again.

"Alive!"

18

"We don't sleep tonight," Nate told Lyons. "We walk straight through."

Crouching in a tangle of black branches, a black wool blanket draped over them like a tent, the three men—Nate, Lyons and Xagil—heard the rotor throb of the helicopter circling the ridge.

Points of sunlight penetrated the weave. Holes in the blanket allowed searing rays of light to slash through the dark interior of their concealment. Nate put an eye to one of the holes.

"Not an army helicopter. Blue and white. Looks like the insignia of a corporation on the side. No weapons. Guatemalans in the front. There's a...white-haired man, an *europerro* in it."

Even with his bad Spanish, Lyons laughed at Nate's pun. The word "*europeo*" meant European in Spanish. The word "*perro*" meant dog. Nate and Lyons shared the same disdain for all non-Americans: English, French, Spanish, Germans, Dutch. "*Europerro*" meant European dog. The noise of the rotor faded. They waited, listening. The sun heated the claustrophobic space, but they made no move to let down the blanket. Outside, Marylena and Juana talked in *Quiche*. Xagil raised one corner of their makeshift concealment. Chill wind swept dust into their faces, the sudden gust making the blanket billow against the branches.

"They say it's gone—" Nate called out in the guttural language. The women answered. Nate did not move. "It's far away. We'll wait until it is gone. And then wait a few more minutes. You know the tricks...."

"It's not the helicopter that scares me," Lyons countered. "It's this trail. This trail is known. It's on the maps. And if it's—"

"No. It is not on the maps. It is known only by the people of these mountains."

"Sorry, but I got the facts in black and white."

Taking his plastic-laminated Xerox from his jacket pocket, Lyons spread out the folds. He maneuvered the map under a shaft of sunlight. Despite the optically reduced scale and the diffusion added by the plastic, the faint lines of mountain trails appeared here and there. With a point of his knife Lyons indicated the ridge where they hid, then traced the intermittent line of the trail along the ridge.

"Where did you get this?"

"One of the offices in D.C. makes these maps from satellite info. I had them project and photocopy a section of a big map and then reduce the scale so it'd be pocket size. I thought I'd do some hiking, so..."

Nate did not answer. The ex-Recon Marine studied the map with total concentration. Xagil twisted and shifted, trying to look at the map, also. Nate talked with the teenager, then passed the map to him.

"Didn't have anything like that when I was in the service."

"They told me the full-size map of Guatemala, at this scale, would be about a hundred yards square. But it's not on paper. It's in digital code. High tech, and all that. You've been up here for years. You don't know about these things."

"But the Nazis wouldn't have that."

"The Nazis got it all. Remember all the equipment from the NSA that we use on the Team? The International in Mexico had it. And in El Salvador, too. You said there was a European in the helicopter? With white hair?"

"Don't think he was old. Looked big."

"The International's got mercs from everywhere. And we've got to assume that the goons chasing us have all the modern tricks. If they've got a map like mine, they'll have a squad on that trail and on any other trail that shows on the map. I say we cut cross-country, make our own trail."

"You don't do that in these mountains. Look at your map. The mountainsides go straight up and down. Where they don't, people have their fields. We go walking through their fields, the militias will stop us."

"No way to avoid the militias?"

"Maybe we can parallel the trail..." Nate took the map back from Xagil.

The women interrupted them. The rotor throb had faded minutes before. Now the women called out and urged them on. Xagil threw back the blanket. Nate talked with his wife as the group gathered their packs. Lyons squinted against the glare and scanned all the directions for the helicopter. Nothing.

"Into the trees!" Nate shouted out as he ran. "Move!" Marylena and Juana followed him, quick-stepping in their ankle-length wrap-around skirts. Both wore the Italian plastic sandals Lyons had given them. Lyons waited a moment, crouching behind a fallen tree, watching the opposite tree line for movement. Xagil called out. Then Nate shouted again, "Move, specialist!"

Turning fast, hurrying, then running, Lyons sprinted into the forest. The others waited at a rock-protected curve in the trail. After the sunlight of the open area, the semidarkness under the trees felt chill.

Nate posted Xagil at the edge of the burn to watch the trail behind them. Juana left the three-year-old Tecun with Marylena. She went a few hundred yards ahead to watch the trail with a 9mm Beretta autopistol. She and Marylena would maintain contact by means of the toy walkie-talkies Lyons had brought. Though intended for children, the CB walkie-talkies had a range of two hundred yards in the open.

"We got two ways," Nate told Lyons. "Either we risk the trail. Or we risk the fields. If we risk the trail, we might see some patrols. Probably sentries watching the trail for guerrillas or bandits. Sit in one place all night and watch. Not aggressive. If we go down lower, walk through the villages and the fields, we will run into patrols. Dogs. Maybe soldiers. Not good."

Now Lyons studied the map. He compared the line of the trail to the line of the dirt road. The trail followed the ridges, cutting along the rims of valleys to switch over to other mountains. The road ran approximately parallel to the trail, but took a lower route, winding along the convolutions and whorls of the mountains, weaving to gain altitude.

Years of action and a few books of theory made one calculation unconscious and automatic. Lyons clicked his mind into predator mode. He mentally became one of the Guatemalan Fascists.

He wanted prisoners. To kill would be easy. Wait, then aim and fire. Or place claymores, then wait. Hit the detonator. But to take a prisoner?

How would *he* take the *norteamericano* alive?

The trail offered infinite ambushes. Every turn, every pine-overhung stretch became an opportunity to take the fugitives. A few soldiers could make the capture.

There might be a few casualties in the units, but soldiers expected danger.

But the road presented a more difficult path to watch. The soldiers mounting the ambush could not expect their targets to pass within reach. The fugitives would be watching the sides of the road. And unlike the soldiers, the *norteamericanos* would have no interest in taking prisoners. They would answer any capture attempt with point-blank fire from their autorifles. Dead soldiers could not prevent the escape of the fugitive *norteamericano*.

Lyons searched the road for a good place to make a capture. He saw his grab-zone immediately.

A long stretch of road preceded a hairpin turn. Two concentric topographic circles represented a steep hill overlooking the straightaway.

A perfect trap. Lookouts on the hill could watch the road with binoculars during the day, and with light-enhancing or infrared electronics at night. The lookouts would spot movement on the road and identify the movement as either nontargets—sheep, cattle, local people—or as the fugitives. Add an advance listening post or audio sensors to detect slow, creeping movement. With positive identification the soldiers waiting in ambush at the curve in the road would have several minutes to prepare to make the seizure.

When the fugitives walked into the grab-zone, they could be hit by tear gas and stun-shock grenades or simply confronted by a circle of soldiers with raised rifles.

Switching back to the role of the fugitive, Lyons mentally sketched a path around the ambush. Once past that straightaway, the road did not offer any other obvious traps, as long as the Nazis wanted to make a capture. If they had decided to kill...

Again Lyons touched the map with the point of his knife. "They want to take you. On the road, this is the best place. If we can get around that tonight, then we can sleep and walk out tomorrow. Or catch a ride on a truck. Whatever. In city clothes no one will know where your wife or sister-in-law are from. And you can pass."

"There's two hours walking between here and where we quit the trail. It'll be dark going down."

"Problem is the trail. Anywhere along here, they could take us. But we need to cover distance on the trail if we're going to dodge this place. I say we risk it. That way we go down the mountain by moonlight—"

"No. You and me. We could do it. No problem. But with two children? The baby cries and we're done. We'll do it in the morning. Stay here, sleep. Start out before dawn."

19

In a private home on one of the side streets of Huehuetenango, Jon Gunther monitored the military frequencies. The hours passed without a sighting or contact, the platoons giving quick and routine reports every hour of their watch.

Gunther waited patiently, listening to the radios, sometimes double-checking a map detail. He had ordered a bed placed in the small living room of the rented house, and from time to time he slept, setting his watch to wake him a minute before the hourly reports. He did not take off his clothes or shoes or his shoulder-holstered pistol. He wanted to move immediately on the first report of a sighting or capture.

Despite its status as the social, economic and administrative centre of the *departamento*, Huehuetenango became quiet after dark. The markets closed in the afternoon. Shops closed at six. The movie theater went dark at ten. Paramilitary police or soldiers stood at every intersection, watching the few passersby, checking identification at random. Though the heaviest fighting of the civil war had been in the Quiche, fighting continued in the north of the *Departamento de Huehuetenango*, where guerrillas infiltrated from

Mexico. No one in the city spoke of the war, but the war cleared the streets early every evening.

Gunther listened to the city go quiet. In the silence a motorcycle could be heard for a few minutes, approaching, passing, then fading into the distance. He heard the squeaking of the boots of the guards pacing the patio of the house. Gunther lay on the dusty bed in the old house and waited.

Waiting tried the resolve of men. In the hours without action, men thought of errors and possible errors, the thousands of combinations of errors leading inevitably to failure. Or disaster. Or disgrace.

Yet Gunther felt no doubts. No fears. No uncertainties.

Years of training, years of action, risking his life, had steeled his nerves. If he had been a man who carried doubts of himself, of his strength and intelligence, of his duty, he would have died of ulcers or heart failure or anxiety—or a bullet. No one could play his double game and survive unless they had a mind like cold, polished steel.

His personal records in the files of the International stated that he had been born in Paraguay in the 1930s of German-immigrant parents. Photocopies of the birth certificates of his parents and their immigration forms established his claim to Aryan purity.

The records went on to detail his early education, his early enthusiasm for the Hitler Youth, then after the war, his devoted service to the hundreds of expatriates enjoying exile in Paraguay. The exiles had fled defeated Germany and needed young intelligent men of unquestioning loyalty to watch for the Israeli agents persecuting the aging Nazis for their service to the

Reich. In a few cases circumstances required the guards to act against Israeli threats. Though the Zionists succeeded in kidnapping Herr Eichmann from Argentina, the zealous young Germans of Paraguay protected their seniors. The young Jon Gunther proved himself again and again.

His loyalty and discipline won the recognition of the Reich veterans too young or too dynamic to accept a quiet life of retirement. From Paraguay and the other nations of South and Central America, the exiled party leaders and veterans of the SS ran worldwide enterprises. Using wealth looted from the people of Europe as capital, the Nazis created syndicates to transport drugs, prostitutes, fugitives, stolen national funds—the traditional exports of South American criminals—north to the United States and Europe. Luxury goods returned, to be sold duty free to the upper classes of Latin America. Often the luxuries became gifts to the administrators who protected the Nazis operating from their nations.

Gunther became a trusted bodyguard. He accompanied his employers to the syndicate meetings, where the dons of the Nazi mafia—much like their Italian, Sicilian and American counterparts in the north—divided the territories and enterprises among themselves. But unlike the gunners of the Mafia, Gunther did not protect his employer from other Nazis. The Nazi lords did not fear one another. True, Gunther and the other guards remained watchful for a possible explosion of psychotic violence from one of the aging wunderkinder of the long-smashed Third Reich, but the real threats came from outside the Aryan cabal.

The Nazi syndicates threatened the traditional domination of international crime by the Hispanic military. Underworld gangs resented the European newcomers. North American Mafia lords wanted the Nazi drug pipelines. All, at one time or another, attacked Gunther's employers. But the worst were the Israelis.

Israeli agents came with a relentless stream of threats. Intelligent, well trained, extremely brave— suicidal!—they slipped into South America, searching for the men who had engineered the near-extermination of the European Jews. The example of Eichmann, succumbing to the bourgeois comforts in Argentina and dying on the gallows in Israel, kept all his comrades moving from nation to nation. And always the Zionist agents followed.

Once the theft of Israeli immigration files provided Gunther with an invaluable education in the Zionist menace. Gunther studied thousands of visa photos and learned that no one could look at a stranger and determine the stranger's race and religion. Blond Jews came from Europe. Red-haired, freckled Jews came from the United States. Hispanic Jews came from Mexico. Black Jews came from Ethiopia.

Anyone might be a Jew.

After all, Gunther himself lived a sham. Though he did possess pure Aryan blood, the Gunthers had not been his parents. They had been the parents of the Jon Gunther born in Paraguay. In the early 1960s, before the Berlin Wall divided east from west, Communist from Federal, the young Jon Gunther had traveled as a tourist to visit his ancestors' homeland. One of his friends in West Germany—who happened to be a Soviet agent—suggested the sentimental journey.

There, in ruined Berlin, as the young man walked the streets of his forefathers, he fell into a dream, a never-waking dream of drugs and small rooms and interrogations continuing for months as doctors speaking German and Spanish took every past experience, every image he had seen, every word he had heard—the total aggregate of his self from his memory. Then came the killing injection and darkness.

The man who adopted Gunther's identity, the new Jon Gunther, had already returned to South America, accepting the opportunity to serve an ex-aide of Goebbels who operated an airline shuttling rich skiers south to the summer snows of the always-white Andes, and the white chemical snow of Bolivia and Peru—cocaine—north to the United States.

The new Jon Gunther rose quickly through the hierarchy. He left behind the few friends who worked as bodyguards. Now he served as a security specialist, no longer protecting only the heads of the syndicates but also the entire syndicates. He reviewed the paramilitary structure of the syndicate security—starting with the credentials of the leader's bodyguards, then the histories and training of the gunmen guarding the enterprise, finally the background of every employee.

Microfilm copies of every document he read went to his superiors in the Soviet KGB. The resources of the world's most comprehensive and most feared intelligence service backed the young analyst. When the Soviet clerks received the information, they double-checked every name, date and place. If a European mercenary had applied for a job, they checked his record against his file in the immense libraries of the KGB. If a *mestizo* gunman listed employment with a drug dealer, the KGB forwarded a request for information to their agents in the FBI, DEA and the CIA.

Jon Gunther came to be known as a meticulous and almost infallible security analyst. His reputation led him to the most ambitious gangster of the hemisphere, the billionaire son of distinguished SS officer, Unomundo.

From his position as chief of security of the International, Gunther directed the military operations of the corporations of Unomundo as the second-generation would-be *Amerikaner Reichführer* expanded his empire through transnational corporate fascism, marketing weapons to the dictatorships of Somoza and Pinochet and Lucas García, cocaine to the democracies, girls to the Arabs, and petrochemical fertilizer to the agribusiness of the hemisphere. His own freighters and air-cargo companies carried his products and his vessels never traveled empty.

When unions demanded medical benefits and wages equaling the cost of living, Unomundo—through his director of security, Colonel Gunther—hired off-duty police officers to maim or kill the leaders. When politicos faced challengers who might impose restrictions or taxes on the corporations of the International, Unomundo assigned sympathetic "state security" officers to purge the opposition. When North American journalists probed the links between politics and profit, Unomundo employed expedient means—murderous street thugs, duplicitous editors or corporate directives—to silence the reports.

Throughout the 1970s Unomundo exploited the turmoil of the decade to multiply his holdings of companies and to amass vast wealth. His Fascist philosophy matched the ruthless policies of the colonels in the nations where he operated. Thousands died for his profits. Pinochet annihilated the liberals and socialists of Chile. Somoza sent every critic of his regime to the firing squads of the Nicaraguan National Guard. The dictators General Lucas García of Guatemala and General Romero of El Salvador left their democratic opposition dismembered along the roadsides and rotting in unknown pits.

But the serious opposition—the Communist Party, the Sandinistas, the PLF, the EGP—survived. They did not threaten the market shares or profits of Unomundo. They remained too far underground to be exterminated by the security services. The militant Communists, the true threats to their nations, endured.

And in this way Gunther served two masters.

He preserved the empire of the International, advancing Unomundo's dream of a Pan-American Reich.

And he advanced the dream of Vladimir Lenin, who foresaw a world Soviet state.

Gunther saw no contradiction in his work. His classes in the theories of socialist progress had thoroughly prepared him for the seeming contradiction of a Nazi creating a hemispherical Fascist regime that would lead to the creation of a world Soviet.

His indoctrination had not included brainwashing or chemical manipulation of his mind. His teachers simply encouraged him to read history.

Had not the Fascist Tzar led to the creation of the first Soviet?

Had not Eastern Europe required invasion and destruction by Hitler before the victory of people's socialism?

Had not the African nations suffered the Europeans and their neocolonial regimes before the victory of the peoples' socialism?

Had not the Americans and General Lon Nol created Pol Pot?

Had not Somoza created the Sandanistas?

Let the idealists and radicals rave of "the inevitable and relentless march of the people to world socialism." Gunther acted to create the world Soviet.

He did this by eliminating liberals, socialists, nationalists—anyone who appealed to voters and the electoral process. He killed them all without discrimination. Under the cover of Unomundo's transnational Fascist profit motive, Gunther liquidated any leader who in a search for election spoke against Unomundo or his allies. If they sought election to serve their people and their country—and not Unomundo's dream of Pan-American fascism—they died.

The election of any leader—radical, conservative, Marxist or Jeffersonian—led to democracy. And democracy led to the creation of opportunity, enterprise, bourgeois wealth—just as in the easy complacent societies of the Western nations.

In bourgeois democratic societies only one election victory remained impossible—no society would vote for the peoples' paradise of communism—the Gulag death camps, the Stalins, the gray regimes of dictatorial bureaucracies.

Only fascism created the chaos required for the formation of Soviet states.

Therefore Gunther worked with Unomundo to destroy any hope of democracy. Unomundo would achieve his Fascist state. Then from the chaos of his neo-Nazi regime the Soviet Union would create the Soviet Republics of the Americas.

And Carl Lyons would play a role.

20

In darkness they rearranged their loads. They worked by touch, not risking penlights except to check critical details.

Lyons secured his pack's compression straps, then shook his pack and listened. Nothing clinked. A few steps away, he heard the small sounds of the infant Quetzal gulping at her mother's breast. He felt a hand touch him.

"You got those pills ready?"

"You sure?"

"If they cry, we'll die. We did it before, when we had to get some children past Unomundo's mercs. But with Seconal. It's safe."

"Cover me up."

Xagil draped a blanket over Lyons as Nate held a flashlight. Sitting cross-legged, using the side of his boot heel as a working surface, Lyons put down a torn-off corner of his map. Then he set a five-milligram tablet of Valium on the plastic-coated paper. He cut the tablet in half. Flicking away one half, he ground the other 2.5 milligrams into a fine powder. Finally he folded the slip of paper into a tight square.

"Here. And tell her to give the kid lots of milk. This is a chemical. It could burn the baby's throat."

"*Claro*—right. Keep it. You're in the light. Here she is—"

Clear plastic Italian sandals appeared under the blanket. Then the black cloth of a wraparound skirt, tight over bent knees. The light went dark for an instant and the blanket swirled.

Her *huipile* split halfway down to her waist, Quetzal at her breast, Marylena knelt in the dirt beside Lyons. In the soft light, holding the sucking child against her, she half smiled to Lyons, her eyes black, one full breast exposed between the brilliant red and purple of her *huipile*. She looked no older than nineteen, her face that of a teenager's but her breasts and baby made her a woman. A Mayan madonna and child.

Nate whispered to her through the blanket and Marylena answered, "*Je, je.*" She repeated her acknowledgment in Spanish for Lyons. "*Si, entiendo, Señor Abaj. Je.*"

Lyons learned his first word of *Quiche*.

Carefully unfolding the scrap of plastic and paper, Lyons reached out to sift the powdered Valium into the baby's mouth. Marylena gently pulled the child from her breast. Streams of milk shot from the teat. Grabbing with her tiny hands, Quetzal tried to pull the breast back.

Despite the danger and the urgency, Lyons felt embarrassed to be staring at Marylena's naked, milk-dripping breast.

Holding the baby in one arm for an instant, Marylena grabbed Lyons's free hand and placed it under Quetzal's head. With Marylena holding the baby in both arms and Lyons holding the baby's head, they managed to keep her still. His fingers pressed against her breast, milk flowing on his hand. Lyons forced himself to ignore his embarrassment. Changing his hold slightly, still supporting the baby's head, he put a finger in the baby's mouth and forced the tooth-stubbed gums apart. This also put the back of his hand against Marylena's breast.

Milk flowed down his hand and wrist. He carefully tapped the grains of powder into the baby's mouth, then slipped his hand free of Marylena's breast. The baby gulped milk, coughed once, then gulped again, swallowing all of the sedative. Marylena smiled to Lyons, then the light went black. He heard her slip away.

Nate laughed softly beside him. "Taste it, it's sweet."

Lyons laughed, too. Holding the light, Nate had watched Lyons's embarrassment and fumbling with the baby and the breast and the drug. Lyons called the dare and licked the back of his hand. The milk did taste sweet.

"Give Tecun at least twice the dose," Nate told him as he pushed the sleepy three-year-old under the blanket.

Rubbing his eyes, Tecun watched as Lyons ground an entire five-milligram tablet. Then Lyons motioned for Tecun to eat the powder. He made a face at the taste but swallowed the Valium. The light went out. Lyons heard fluid sloshing in a plastic bottle and then Tecun drank.

Nate and Xagil whispered to each other, then one of the women answered. Nate passed the penlight to Lyons.

"Juana has a trick to make," Nate told him.

Both Xagil and Nate held up blankets while Lyons held the penlight for Juana. Sitting in the dirt, she loosely stitched neat folds into a blanket, creating what looked like a casually folded blanket. Then she slipped her Uzi into the blanket. She pulled it out, slipped it in. The blanket served as concealment. Lyons noticed that Juana wore headphones.

As she worked she listened to music on a cassette player. Lyons looked to Nate and pointed at the headphones and tape player. Nate grinned.

"Mayans are crazy about technology."

"She can't play it when we're moving."

"She's not that crazy."

Juana made a second folded blanket to conceal a Galil. With the steel tubing stock folded forward, the blanket concealed the autorifle.

"She will carry one blanket in her hands," Nate explained. "Xagil carries the other one."

Juana rolled a second blanket into a bundle, then folded her *tzute* around the rolled blanket. Tying the ends of the cloth around her body, she created the illusion of a baby.

Lyons understood. With a blanket in her hands and carrying a baby on her back, she would look like thousands of other Mayan women, rising before dawn to begin another day in their lifelong cycle of work and child care; they are women who quit the day's labor only when sunlight or kerosene failed.

"Got your pack here?" Nate asked.

"Yeah, I'm ready to move."

"No, you aren't. You think Tecun's walking? You carry him." Nate spoke quickly to his son and the boy stumbled a few steps away.

"Sure, whatever. What happens if there's—"

"Then you get my son out of it. Understand?"

"I understand."

In the graying darkness Tecun took a quick piss. Returning to Lyons, he wormed into the backpack. Lyons pulled the compression straps tight. Feeling the shape of the boy inside, he found that Tecun had converted his gear and clothes into a seat. Only Tecun's head showed outside.

Lyons pulled on the straps and stood. Not bad. Tecun weighed not much more than thirty pounds. He took his rifle and started out. Behind him he heard Tecun laugh.

"Va! –Va, mi caballo!"

"I'm not your horse, kid!"

They moved in single file, Juana and Xagil a hundred yards ahead. At the first bend in the trail, they tested the CB walkie-talkies. The mountainside cut the signal, but Nate understood his sister-in-law's words. She could relay a warning.

Then they moved fast, almost jogging along the trail. Juana and Xagil maintained the pace, staying far ahead. From time to time, when the trail doubled back in the fold of a mountain, Lyons saw them, two shadows moving through the predawn darkness. Above the pines the darkness became violet. Pines became black columns and networks of shatter-patterns. Birds flitted through the higher branches, the first territorial calls ringing out in the forest.

Lyons heard birds that seemed no more than an arm's distance away. Good, he thought. A threatened bird flies or goes silent. If we're so quiet that the birds don't hear us, maybe we've got a chance.

But he knew, if a tough unit of soldiers waited on the trail ahead, watching for them, they had no chance. The soldiers would let the *indígenas* pass, then jump the *norteamericanos*.

Maybe they're sleeping on watch, Lyons thought. Maybe they aren't up there, maybe they don't like to hike and they're waiting on the highway.

Let nothing happen here, Lyons prayed. Not with Nate's boy on my back and Nate's wife and baby five steps ahead. God, Jehovah, Jesus, Allah, Buddha, Quetzalcoatl, Tolque Nahuaque, Mary Immaculate, Tonanzin, Electromagnetism, God-of-the-Swirling-Infinite-Stars, Spirits of the Mountain, the Forest, Spirits I don't Even Know About—let me get my friend and his family out. Take me some other day, when I'm alone. I'm your meat, not these innocent little kids.

His senses seemed to expand into a sphere of all-awareness. Fear defined every sound, every shape, every shadow. The forest around him assumed the false dimension and depth of a three-dimensional print, the blue behind the pines becoming the color of dread because the light meant day, day when the soldiers would get an easy sight-image over their rifles.

The plastic grips of the Galil in his hands became slick with his sweat. Ahead of him Marylena struggled to keep the pace. Lyons saw that the plastic sandals gave the sides of her feet no protection. Hurrying in the half light, she had already cut her feet on the trail's rocks.

If they follow us with dogs, her blood will smell like raw meat.

No time to help her. Make distance!

Every branch and bush overhanging the trail made Lyons's body surge with adrenaline. Will this be it? What happens when they see two *norteamericanos*?

A stream. A rivulet of clear water ran down the mountainside's stones. Lyons glanced up. Daylight lighted hundreds of yards of sheer mountain above them. He saw translucent blue sky and the swirl of clouds.

The idea came, take care of Marylena's feet. Lyons hissed to Nate, "Stop!"

"Why?" Nate rushed back to him.

"Marylena's feet. She's ripping up her feet. She won't be able to keep up if she—"

"She ripped up her feet yesterday and she'll rip them up today. We got no time."

"They might have dogs! I wash the blood off here and they won't—"

"Yeah. Do it. Fast." Nate whispered to his wife, and she sat at the side of the trickling water.

Lyons moved fast, shrugging out of his pack. Tecun had fallen into a drugged sleep. Pulling out clothes and adhesive tape, Lyons went to work. He washed her feet and sandals, dried them with one of his shirts, then looped two-inch-wide adhesive tape around her feet, covering the cuts, the soles, her feet, binding the sandals to her feet. Then he slipped a pair of his heavy hiking socks over her feet, pulled them tight, then taped the socks in place.

White tape crisscrossing the dark-blue socks, a solid band of tape at each ankle, her new footwear looked like trash. But the two layers of tape and the socks would protect her feet. The resoling had taken only three minutes. Lyons jammed the tape and shirt back into the pack and moved, buckling up as he ran to catch up with Nate and Marylena.

He glanced down at her new footprints. The soft socks left only a blurry smear on the sand.

The trail cut up the mountainside, then angled to a ridge. Nate broke into a run to close the distance to Juana and Xagil.

Then Nate stopped. Going flat on the trail, he motioned with his open hand. Marylena stopped. With fear in her eyes she looked from her husband to Lyons as he crept past her. Checking his rifle's safety out of habit, Lyons went into a slow crouchwalk, finally going flat behind Nate. He inched up as he whispered, "What goes on?"

"Soldiers have got them."

The side of his face in the dirt, Lyons peered through the dry grass and brush. The trail passed through a sunlit patch of grass. A group of soldiers in camo fatigues stood around Juana and Xagil. Only one of them pointed a rifle at Xagil, but the others all held Galils. Xagil casually held the folded blanket under his left arm as he gestured ahead with his right.

"He's telling them that they're going to the road, to take a bus. They want to know what's in the blankets...."

Lyons heard the safety of Nate's Galil click down as Nate hissed, "I take left to right, you right to left—"

And he fired. Lyons saw faces over the sights of his Galil and he dropped a soldier, then another and another. Autofire ripped, an Uzi went wild in long, scything bursts. Lyons shot everything that wore camouflage.

Not bothering to pull her weapon clear of the blanket, Juana emptied her Uzi at the soldiers and rushed off the trail, jerking Xagil behind her. He fell backward into the brush, firing his Galil at the mountainside above them. Concealed soldiers returned the fire.

As Nate continued shooting, Lyons scrambled backward, Tecun crying on his back. Valium did not have enough sedative effect to keep the child asleep through a firefight. Lyons put his rifle down for an instant and pulled Tecun off his back. He left the crying boy with his mother and sister, then slung his Galil over his shoulder and climbed straight up the mountainside.

The firing died down to aimed bursts and single shots. Wounded soldiers screamed, other soldiers shouted. A grenade banged. Lyons moved fast and quiet, ignoring the branches tearing at his face and hands. Rocks tumbled down behind him.

At the crest of the sharp ridge, he looked down on the trail. Soldiers sprawled on the dirt and rocks, blood pooling around them. Above the grab-zone, other soldiers shifted positions, firing on Nate. From his position Lyons saw it all.

Don't fight, win, Lyons thought, adrenaline beating at his brain. He forced himself to think, to go slow. Win. And winning means killing all these soldiers without getting hurt. You get wounded and you can't help your friend. You'll die in these mountains. And maybe Nate and Marylena and the kids, too. Winning means life.

He crawled slowly, carefully placing his hands and feet, not dislodging dirt or rocks. Paralleling the trail for twenty or thirty yards, he angled down as he neared the soldiers. Between the shots he heard a soldier thrashing through the brush.

The teenager had the same idea as his opponent, Carl Lyons. But too late. Glancing below him to check the positions of the other soldiers, Lyons shouldered his Galil and fired a round through the boy's head. As the body fell Lyons slid down, firing bursts into the backs of other soldiers.

Then he saw what he had feared: a soldier shouting into a field radio. Lyons fired wild, spraying rounds through the soldier's head and hands and the radio, brains exploding, plastic and metal flying from shattered radio.

Silence. His ears ringing, Lyons listened for the movement of other soldiers. But he heard no movement, no firing, only the groaning of the dying.

And crying. Thirty yards away, where the trail crossed the ridge, he heard Marylena sobbing and crying out. Xagil broke cover and rushed to her. Juana waved to Lyons, then she stepped out on the trail. She fired a 2-shot burst into the head of every soldier on the ground.

"Señor Abaj!" Xagil shouted out. *"Viene!"*

Lyons quickly checked the soldiers he had shot. Dead. But the radio message had gone out. He slid down to the trail and ran to the ridge.

Cursing in three languages, blood flowing through his hands, Nate held his bullet-shattered leg.

21

As the noise and panic of the firefight came from the radio, Colonel Gunther found the position of platoon one on the map. A red triangle marked a point on the mountain trail, a few miles north of where he had seen the two women the previous afternoon. Gunther listened as the desperate young man described the action:

"An Indian woman with a baby...walking with a boy, they had guns hidden in blankets...other guerrillas hit us...many of us dead...we killed two...there's shooting behind...a *norteamericano*, the blond *norteamericano*, the one in the description, he's—"

Gunther heard point-blank autofire, an instant of an electronic shriek, then static. He tried to fine-tune the frequency. Nothing. Only static.

Carl Lyons had finally appeared. As usual, he had first deceived his opponents, this time with the device of wandering *indígenas*. The soldiers waiting in ambush had questioned two passing *indígenas*, therefore revealing their trap. Then in his usual way, Lyons liquidated his opponents with daredevil—yet intelligent and classical—attacks.

No one could call Lyons less than a phenomenon. Gunther knew Lyons. Lyons had eliminated several units either allied with the International or directly commanded by officers of the International. In the Quiche disaster Lyons had led a force that succeeded in killing a thousand mercenaries and wounded Unomundo himself. In California Lyons had pursued a Salvadoran death squad and exterminated the unit. In El Salvador he had assaulted the fortress-plantation of Colonel Roberto Quesada, forced the colonel to flee to Honduras, then done the impossible—raided an International training center, devastated the installation and escaped—with a force of only ten or fifteen men, aided by a single DC-3 cargo plane.

And in Mexico, Lyons had captured Gunther himself. Shot out of the sky, pursued across the desert by overwhelming numbers of Mexican soldiers, Lyons had turned on his opponents and destroyed them. He continued his campaign against the International not by attacking the nearest base, from where the pursuing units had been dispatched, but by hijacking a helicopter and suddenly appearing two thousand miles away and attacking the command center. The devastation of the high-rise offices of the International did not enhance Unomundo's reputation as the omnipresent and always-victorious leader.

Yet the Mexican defeat had led to this opportunity. Gunther, as the prisoner of Able Team, had talked with Lyons day after day. And he had seen the contradictions within the American—the idealistic antiterrorist crusader now an embittered terrorist himself; a man obsessed by his mission who had been betrayed by those who dispatched him on his mission; a man fighting without respite for years against not only foreign and Soviet forces, but also forces of his own country.

Lyons fought everyone.

He found a target, he destroyed it.

Nothing stopped him except the absence of enemies.

Gunther, in his years of work with soldiers and mercenaries and assassins, had seen the syndrome before.

Lyons had become a self-guided weapon rampaging through the maze of realpolitik.

Terrorism enraged Lyons. He had no sense of history and dialectic, therefore he attacked terrorists.

Communism enraged Lyons. He had no sense of the inevitable, therefore he attacked Communists.

Fascists, criminals, gangsters, religious psychotics—Lyons did not appreciate their place in the dynamics of history, therefore he killed them all.

His unending rage, his projection of righteousness onto a world of chaos and apparently meaningless atrocity, his obsession to right a world that had never and would never be right all made Lyons a dangerous man—if he was against you.

Lyons belonged to another time. Gunther realized he would miss Carl Lyons after he had used him. But then, if Gunther survived his own career to retire, perhaps he could write a dissertation on the American Quixote. But that would be far in the future....

With the calm of a pianist playing a long-rehearsed score and reaching out to strike a resounding chord, Gunther telephoned the army base and ordered the preparation of his helicopter.

Today Gunther would make Lyons his weapon.

22

Entering the back of his thigh at 3,300 feet per second, the 5.56mm bullet had exploded through his muscles, shattering the bone. Fragments of bone and metal had deflected wildly through the muscles and veins, the main mass of bone and deaccelerating metal fragments continuing through his leg to exit a hand's width above his knee. Though the bullet had not severed the femoral artery—if it had, he would have died within two minutes—Nate could not move. And that meant he would die there.

Nate knew it. Lyons knew it.

But Lyons wadded pads of cloth against the entrance and exit wounds and taped the pads in place as he shouted to Xagil, "*Palos!* Sticks!"

The teenager only stared, either not understanding Lyons or too shocked by the inevitable death of his cousin. Lyons pantomimed sticks for splints on each side of the flopping leg. Understanding, the teenager ran to find the wood.

Marylena sobbed and clutched at her husband. Nate spoke slowly and calmly to her, his face white with pain. He reached up and touched her tears with one hand, then with the other arm pulled Tecun down

against him and hugged him. He talked past Marylena to Juana, questioning her.

Lyons understood none of the *Quiche*. He worked
to stablilize the wound, to stop the bleeding, using a
pair of his pants as a pressure band over the pads.
There might be a chance, somehow. Xagil returned
with two snapped-off branches. Lyons took them,
then sent him out again for a longer branch, one that
would go from Nate's waist to his ankle.

Nate glanced at the work on the wound, then spoke
to Lyons. "Surprise, Señor Abaj. Guess what Juana
tells me? They're looking for two gringos—me and
you. They know about you. So forget about playing
tourist if any soldiers stop you."

"Any soldiers stop us, they've got big problems."

"Us? You mean you and the others."

"And you—"

"Not me." Nate pointed to the embankment overlooking the trail. "I want you to take me up that hillside and set me up. For my last stand."

"No. I'm getting you out."

"Forget it. No way to do it. Do what I say."

"I won't leave you here to die."

"I'd do the same for you, specialist. I'm staying
here. That clearing, their helicopter will come down
there. I'll hit them. Give you time."

"I'll tie you onto my back. Xagil can carry Tecun.
I can carry you out."

Nate laughed. Then his hand whipped up and
grabbed Lyons's shirt. He jerked Lyons down to face
him. "I can't make it out! I am dead! You will do
what I say. You will get my wife and baby and my boy
out, or I will come back from hell and scream in your

head until you die shaking. Now face the fact and get with it. I will give you time.''

Putting an arm under Nate, Lyons pulled the man against him for a moment. He felt a sob catch in his throat. "I'll get them out. If I can—''

The hoarse voice shouted in his ear. "None of that *if* shit. Even if you're only a Washington, D.C., hotshot, think like a marine. Do the impossible. You hear me? Now quit the tear-jerk scene and pack me up.''

Lyons broke the embrace. He looked up to see Xagil with a length of pine. The boy also had several belts taken from the fatigues of the dead soldiers. Nate held his wife and gave Lyons instructions.

"There's a couple of those *puto*-squad claymores in my pack. There's det-cord and a mechanical striker. I'm going to rig a dead man's surprise. After they kill me or after I bleed to death, they'll try to drag me off and that'll be my funeral plan. Nothing left for the dogs to eat. God, I'm glad I never taught Marylena English.''

Speaking past Lyons, Nate talked quickly with Xagil. Xagil nodded and ran to the dead soldiers. Lyons saw him gathering ammunition and grenades.

"You're ready to go," Lyons told him, his voice emotionless, as he cinched tight the last belt. The three lengths of wood and the several belts made the mangled leg immobile and straight. "I'm sorry, Nate. I didn't move fast enough up there. I didn't get them before they shot you.''

"Shut up. Quit the melodrama. Quit the confessions. You're going to live. Drag me up there. The Nazi fuck-shits are on their way.''

Xagil took one arm, Lyons the other. Despite the splints, Nate screamed and cursed as they dragged him over the ground. Marylena sobbed and followed, crying out to her husband, holding their baby in one arm and clutching at his shirt with the other hand.

Working together, Lyons and Xagil pulled Nate up the steep embankment. They placed him so that he could stay on his back and fire down into the helicopter's landing zone. "Give me my pack. Load rifles and stack them here. Get that FN squad gun. Pull those dead ones over here. Let them stop a few bullets for me. Break off some branches for camouflage. Now get out of here. You're wasting time."

Lyons shoved Xagil down the embankment. He slipped after him without looking back. Getting his rifle and pack, he heard Marylena shrieking. Juana pulled her sister away, shaking her, pointing to the baby she held, to her son. Nate shouted down from the hillside, and finally, like an automaton, Marylena positioned her daughter in the *tzute* on her back. And staggered away.

Carrying Tecun in her arms, Juana ran to Lyons. Wordlessly they zipped the boy into the backpack. Then they jogged after the others.

Invisible in the tangle of piled branches, Nate called out to Lyons, "Sorry for talking tough. I had to. Or you'd do something stupid."

"No problem. *Adios.*"

"Get my family out."

"No ifs. I'll do it."

"And I promised them you would take them to the United States. Don't break my promise."

"You got it. No ifs. *Adios*, Nate."

"You, too, spookman."

At the edge of the clearing, Marylena looked back, her face streaming tears, her mouth slack with grief. Lyons slapped her shoulder with the palm of his hand, spinning her away. She stumbled after her sister.

As the others ran, Lyons took the time to rip a long branch from a tree. He gave Nate a last wave, then ran, pulling the branch behind him to obliterate their tracks. He did not want the react unit to know their numbers. Maybe they'd think a gang of fugitives wiped out the ambush squad.

They ran, covering ground without pause. Xagil ran point. Juana helped Marylena along, coaxing her, comforting her, jerking her along when she slowed. Last in line, Lyons stopped from time to time to look at the map, studying the topographic whorls and comparing the lines and swirls to the landscape around her. Then he rushed to catch up with the others. The branch he dragged scoured the trail clean of tracks. From minute to minute he expected to hear approaching helicopters.

Lyons wondered if Nate could give them enough time. And what if he slowed the react squads for a few minutes? So what if he killed three or four soldiers? There had to be units ahead somewhere. In the mountains, on the road north, on the highway.

Then as he ran, his eyes skimming the pines and mountainsides for signs of an ambush, he realized he had another option.

The soldiers in the ambush unit had not suspected Xagil and Juana. Disregarding the first rule of ambush, they had left their positions to question two passing local people about the two *norteamericanos*.

They had seen Xagil and Juana as possible sources of information, not fugitives. Juana told Nate that the soldiers had described two foreigners. But the soldiers had not thought the two foreigners traveled with *indígenas*.

That lack of information had killed the squad. And that missing information might keep Nate's family alive.

Meeting a sheer mountainside, the trail veered to the left. Xagil ran a hundred yards east before Lyons's whistle stopped him. According to the map, the trail turned west for a mile. There, it ran up the mountain, passed over the ridge, then down the opposite slope.

However, if they cut east, leaving the trail and climbing over a parallel ridge, then dropping down the steep mountainside, they would find the road. More important, they would come down to the north of where Lyons and Nate had agreed would be the perfect ambush zone.

In his terrible Spanish Lyons explained this to Xagil, who then explained to Juana. Marylena knelt a few steps away from the others, crying and rocking her baby, singing a quiet song of mourning.

Lyons took the time to confirm what Nate had told him. In three-or four-word questions in Spanish he asked: "The soldiers look for me? The soldiers do not look for you?" "The soldiers do not look for *indígenas* with me?"

Xagil answered *si* to all the questions, explaining in great detail exactly what the soldiers had said and done before the shooting started. Lyons understood almost nothing of what Xagil told him, and Lyons finally told him to get going.

Moving again, Xagil led the women up the mountainside. Above them, clouds streamed over the ridges. Lyons stayed behind a moment to brush their footprints from the trail's dust, then he followed them, taking a different angle up the mountainside. Swirls of chill, misty air drifted through the forest.

He wished he could erase the marks of their passing from the forest matting of leaves and moss and small plants. But he couldn't. A branch obscured a footprint left in dirt; nothing could regenerate crushed grass and ferns but time. So if soldiers followed, he wanted them to think they pursued several fugitives. That would slow them down.

Gain time. He rushed ahead of the others, his pulse hammering with the exertion of the climb and the weight of Tecun in his pack. Ahead of Xagil and the women, he waved them past, then doubled back, making more tracks. If soldiers followed them up this slope, those soldiers wouldn't know what to expect. Make them think a group went to the top and divided up. He thought of leaving a grenade as a booby trap, but if the soldiers didn't trip it, a woodcutter might.

Lyons rushed up the mountain, gasping, choking, hawking out his lungs. At first he thought he heard the self-destruction of his heart, his heartbeat drumming to a crescendo before the involuntary muscles died from stress. He staggered to the crest. A moment of wind-driven cloud struck him like a breaking wave. He stood in the white void, gulping down the wonderfully cold, moist air. The cloud passed. He stood in glaring daylight.

With a hiss Xagil motioned him down. Then Lyons identified the sound. Not his heart. Distant rotor throb, getting louder, approaching, the cycles of the rotors coinciding, resonating into a single drumbeat of doom.

Dodging into the pines, Lyons glanced at the shadows to orient himself, then looked back in the direction of Nate. Trees and swirls of drifting cloud blocked his sight. Lyons ran along the ridge. He found a good angle for viewing the landscape to the south.

Two specks approached. One dark, the other white. As he watched, the dark speck became an OD Huey troopship, the other a blue-and-white civilian model. Sunlight flashed from the corporate helicopter's polish.

Within a minute the helicopter reached a point a few miles away and circled around what Lyons assumed to be the position of the dead squad.

Lyons twisted to look over his shoulder. Tecun slept. Lyons found a place where he could watch what would happen on the mountainside to the south. He would not lose much time by watching, and some day the story would be very important.

It would be over fast. Lyons—if he survived— wanted to be able to tell Tecun how his father died.

23

As the troopship circled the landing zone, ex-Colonel Morales studied the clearing beneath him. Dead soldiers were sprawled everywhere on the trail, their camouflage dark against the yellow dust. Some of the men had pools of blood around their heads. The *norteamericanos* had executed the wounded with bullets to the brains. When the circling movement took the helicopter away from the mountainside, he saw the forms of soldiers in the green of the hillside overlooking the trail. Nothing moved.

Guatemalan soldiers loyal to the International filled the troopship. Like himself, they looked down at their dead compatriots. No one spoke or gestured. They gripped their rifles and watched the scene beneath them, their faces impassive, set. Even the door gunner did not move, his hands locked on his Heckler and Koch 7.62mm MG-3, only his eyes moving as he looked for the *norteamericanos* who had wiped out the squad.

For this action Morales had returned to the uniform of the Republic and he carried a custom-finished Galil SAR, the short model of the standard army-issue assault rifle. But his tailored and pressed camouflage fatigues bore the eagle and twin lightning strikes of the International.

Morales glanced into the sky. The pilot of the blue-and-white corporate helicopter maintained a distance. Flipping on the aircraft-bank switch, Morales spoke into the com-mike of his headset.

"Colonel Gunther. Nothing is alive down there. The bastards murdered all the wounded before they ran. I will take the men in and begin the hunt for—"

"No!" The word came sharply. "Do not use that landing zone. It will be a trap."

"I will order the men to fire into the area. We will know very quickly if—"

"No! I tell you, Morales, I know this—"

"Colonel Morales," the Guatemalan corrected.

"Yes, Colonel. I tell you, Colonel Morales, I know this man. If you take your men there, you risk your life and the life of every soldier."

"What can one or two men do? They are running. They will not be there. I am—"

"What can they do? Look! You said you saw only death. You ask me what one or two men—"

"I will brief you in a few minutes." Morales ended the argument by flipping off the transceiver switch.

Morales refused to accept orders from the foreigner. As a liaison officer, Gunther could not give him orders, only suggestions. And Morales did not accept the suggestions. Though Gunther objected to the risk, Morales reasoned, he would respect success. He would report to his commander that Morales fearlessly led his men into the action. This would be his opportunity to redeem his reputation with his leader, Unomundo, to demonstrate that his capture two years before had come only due to betrayal.

In fact Morales hoped for a trap. He would distinguish himself. Overwhelm the gringo bastards. Charge directly into their guns and shoot to wound. That is, he would inspire his men to charge directly into the guns. He would fire tear-gas grenades at the gringos while his soldiers distracted their aim.

He would make the capture of the gringo bastard. His victory would be his glory and his vindication.

Flipping on the intercom, he spoke to the pilots. "Circle low! The machine gun will work the place over."

"But it could be an ambush, Colonel. This is a million-dollar aircraft and one bullet could—"

"Shut up! Do as I say! You are under my command!"

Straining against the safety webbing holding him in his seat, Morales reached out and slapped the pressed-steel barrel shroud of the H&K machine gun. The door gunner looked at the colonel, then his eyes went wide with disbelief as the colonel pointed to the tree line around the clearing.

The other soldiers looked at one another. Rotor noise denied them any chance to voice their objections. The descent of the helicopter cut off any mutiny. Soldiers on the door gunner's side accepted the inevitable and joined in the prepping, raising their rifles.

Machine gun and rifle fire tore through the brush surrounding the clearing. Branches and leaves fell, dust rose. The soldiers didn't fire into the areas where the bodies lay. They would not risk killing any man who had miraculously survived.

Men on the far side of the helicopter used the orbits of the landing zone to dump their specially issued tear-gas grenades. They considered the heavy and nonlethal canisters worthless. Rather than carry the weight of the canisters through the mountains for the rest of the day, they pulled the pins and threw the canisters randomly out the side door.

No one returned the fire.

After hundreds of rounds of ammunition had been spent on the trees, the helicopter descended. The door gunner continued firing, aiming bursts into bushes and far above the trail where the pines created deep shadows. Now soldiers fired their rifles from both side doors. They aimed into any cover—the rocks below the LZ, the trees, the slight rise to the south of the clearing, even into the dense branches of trees towering over the trail. One soldier fitted a rifle grenade on his Galil and launched it into a tangle of brush and fallen branches to the north of the clearing.

Still no one fired at the helicopter.

Dust swirled up from the earth. The camouflage uniforms of the dead men on the trail and in the brush above the trail whipped and flapped in the sudden windstorm. As the helicopter's steel skids touched the earth, soldiers leaped down. The colonel followed them, his short Galil held ready.

Men ran into the brush, searching for fugitives. Beyond the clearing tear gas swirled through the pines. Soldiers coughed and cursed, but they found no *norteamericanos* waiting in ambush. Colonel Morales signaled the pilot to cut the engine.

In the swirling dust and rotor noise the burst of automatic-rifle fire seemed muted. Colonel Morales looked around to see who had fired and at what. Then he realized that the bullets tore past him.

Plexiglas fell from the windshield of the helicopter, the plastic crazing, falling in sections as slugs crisscrossed the pilots. Strapped in their seats, the men lurched and screamed and died as heavy 7.62mm slugs from a squad automatic rifle continued smashing through the Plexiglas.

The soldiers fired wild, trying to kill the unseen enemy. But the weapon had already quit, the rifle fire dying away as the soldiers changed magazines and searched for a target. Silence came to the forest as the rotors swooshed slowly to a stop.

Dust drifted. Colonel Morales sprawled in the stubby dry grass, his eyes searching the mountainside for the *norteamericano*. He saw only the dead men in the brush.

A soldier flew back, the shot coming simultaneously, all the other soldiers firing, their wild autofire ripping the pines and the brush of the mountainside. They did not see the sniper, but they knew he must be up there, somewhere.

Colonel Morales felt fear like never before. The sniper had a high position on the mountain. He could fire down on the clearing. The dry grass around the colonel did not conceal him. In fact, his camouflage contrasted the yellow grass, making him stand out like a center ring on a paper target.

His body quivering, he waited for the sniper's next kill, knowing that would be his chance, hoping he did not take the next bullet.

A beret and section of skull flew from a soldier's head, the shot triggering another roar of wild rifle fire. Morales sprinted for the protection of the pines, stumbled, felt stone gouge one knee, ran again, then branches ripped his chest and arms as he threw himself behind a pine. The rifle fire continued.

Other soldiers caught in the open had tried to make the pines. One had not succeeded. He thrashed and screamed in the open, clutching at the bloody ruin of his gut. Soldiers shouted to one another.

Dashing from cover, a soldier hurled a canister at the mountainside and zigzagged back to cover. Then a rifle grenade popped.

Two puffs of white tear gas clouded from the pines. The nonlethal gas now proved its value. Bullets had not found the sniper, but the gas forced him to betray himself.

In the quiet they heard coughing. Muffled, but audible, it came not from high on the mountainside, but low, from among the bodies of their compatriots. Individual shots searched for the sniper, then other men sprinted out with gas canisters.

One man did not survive to make his throw, but his killing the soldier revealed the sniper's exact position, the muzzle blast moving the leaves of a bush.

The soldiers saturated the area with autofire, another soldier staggering back from a pine with blood jetting from his arm, then two rifle grenades arced into the sniper's position.

Again, there was silence.

Gas swirled through the brush and pines. Colonel Morales heard no coughing now. A soldier rushed to the embankment and took cover. No shots had come.

The soldier tossed another gas canister into the place from where the sniper had fired.

They all waited as the tear gas proved the death of the *norteamericano*. A soldier ran into the center of the clearing and bent over the gut-shot man. He had already died. Across the clearing, soldiers put a tourniquet on the shattered arm of the other wounded man.

A dead gringo, Morales thought. But no prisoner. No victory to announce to his leader Unomundo.

Yet only one man had fired. Only one man had died. Which one? The scum that had associated with the *indígenas*? Or the blond one, the specialist that Gunther wanted?

Perhaps he could still find victory in this slaughter.

Seeing two soldiers already searching for the sniper, Colonel Morales ran to the trail, then scrambled up the embankment. A soldier lifted away a branch to expose the corpses.

The dark-haired, dark-skinned *norteamericano* had used the bodies of two soldiers as armor. But bullets and shrapnel had found him, dotting his legs with holes, slashing his face and arms, covering him with his own and other men's gore. He still gripped a Galil. Other rifles and an FAL light machine gun lay beside him.

"Look," one of his men pointed. "That leg. Splinted up like that. He got shot bad. Crippled. So he stayed to fight alone...."

The other soldier nodded. "No hope. But he fought."

"Brave one," the soldier admitted.

"He's a goddamned bastard!" Colonel Morales shrieked, his voice cracking with stress and delayed panic. "A whoreson bastard gringo and I'll take his *balls* home in my pocket. Get that piece of *shit* down from here so we can get him in the other helicopter—"

The soldiers only looked at the colonel, their faces showing contempt for his histronics. So the colonel reached down and grabbed the mangled corpse of the *norteamericano* and pulled him upright....

24

After the distant pops of rifle fire faded, Lyons waited. The wind drove cold moments of cloud past him. The blue-and-white corporate helicopter orbited the LZ at a distance, staying just over a mile—extreme rifle range—away from the action.

Xagil stood behind Lyons. They had seen nothing of the fight, only the circling of the corporate helicopter. After the descent of the troopship the rotor noise had faded. Then came the volleys of rifle and machine gun fire.

The rising and falling of the noise had told the story, the silence the end.

"Is he dead?" Xagil asked, his voice quiet.

A flash. Dust billowed from the forest, rolling over the pines like a breaking wave. Flame exploded an instant later, a great churning ball of fire and black smoke rising straight into the blue sky. The boom echoed through the mountains.

"Yeah, Nate's dead."

Lyons looked back at the face of the sleeping Tecun, the child's dark features and black hair the image of his father and mother superimposed. Now the boy had only his mother.

White void enveloped Lyons and Xagil. Two steps away, Xagil became only a shadow within the white. Lyons heard the teenager sing phrases of the same Quiche song of mourning his mother had sung earlier. When the cloud passed, they saw the corporate helicopter fly straight to the flaming LZ, sweep through a hard recon orbit, then gain altitude. Slowly circling the area, the pilot found another clearing and descended.

The chase was on. Whoever had landed in that helicopter and whoever survived the blast would be after them, on foot or by air. Lyons ran to Juana and signaled her to move. Juana and Xagil helped Marylena down the incline. Hands linked, they stumbled and slid, then they disappeared in the pines and mist as gravity pulled them down.

Checking the map, Lyons mentally plotted the next few miles. He glanced at the mountain to the north, then to the landmarks in the east. The slope of this north-south mountain ended at the twisting road. The road cut through valleys and low hills to meet the east-west highway.

A distance of no less than twelve miles. Through territory controlled by the army of the International—mercenaries, Guatemalan army traitors and corrupt police. Every step subject to ambush or roadblock or airborne observation. Every step taken with desperation and fear as Xagil and Juana led him out of the mountains.

The International wanted Lyons.

They had soldiers waiting in ambush for him, searching for him, questioning the local people.

Anyone—soldier, policeman, bus driver or *campesino*—who saw Lyons would betray him.

And if any informer or soldier saw the family of Quicheneros with Lyons, the family died.

If Lyons wanted to get Nate's family to safety, he had to let them go alone.

But without them, without Xagil and Juana showing him the foot trails and back roads, translating the languages, could he escape the search? Would his xeroxed satellite map guide him out?

No.

This time, he didn't make it. Lyons accepted it. Nate had died so that Lyons and his family had a chance. He had only asked that Lyons get his family out.

Lyons would keep his promise. But he would not go with them.

The decision made, he finally followed the others, running and boot skiing down the steep slope, flashing through shadows and clouds, using his big boots to obscure as many of their footprints as possible. Now he needed to conceal numbers.

In a few minutes he gained on Marylena and Juana. He called out to them to stop, then continued a few hundred yards further and stopped Xagil.

Crouching in the mist-chilled shadows of the pines, Lyons slipped off his backpack. Tecun still slept. Then in simple Spanish sentences repeated many times, he explained what they had to do to escape.

"Give me all the weapons," he explained, pointing to the Uzi and Galil and the pistols. Then he pointed at the cassette player, the walkie-talkies, their shoes—everything from North America. "If the soldiers stop you, they will see nothing different, you will have nothing to betray you.''

Gently, he took Tecun from his pack and gave the boy to Juana. She rolled the boy in a blanket and slung him across her shoulder. He continued sleeping.

Then Lyons cut the adhesive tape off Marylena's feet. As he took the shoes off her cut feet, he explained why. Who would have this tape and these big socks but a *norteamericano*? Who would give *indígenas* beautiful Italian shoes but a *norteamericano*? They would die if they kept his stupid gifts. Better that they walk barefoot like all the other *indígena* women.

On a slip of paper Lyons wrote a long telephone number. The Washington, D.C., area code, followed by a series of access numbers that would route the call through security to Stonyman. He pantomimed how to key the touch tone after the operator made the connection. He stressed that they should not mention Nate's name during the call.

''Say only, 'Señor Stone. The tourist.' Nothing more!''

Give the man at the other end your hotel address. Then don't go back to that hotel. Use a phony name and rent a room at another hotel. Wait there. One of you watch the other hotel. You know my friends. You saw them two years ago. If anyone else comes, run away.''

Though the three Quicheneros understood the complex directions, they did not realize what the directions implied until Lyons gave them his money. He emptied his money belt of thousands of quetzal notes—he had intended to stay for weeks, spending money like water—and dealt out the money like playing cards, dividing the stack of money three ways. Ones, fives, tens, twenties, finally hundreds. He kept none for himself.

Looking at the stack of money in her hand, Juana realized that if the *norteamericano* gave away all his money, then he did not think he would be needing money. Lyons watched the realization dawn on her. She spoke quickly to Xagil. Both tried to give the money back to him.

Marylena looked at him, glancing down at the money, then talking with her sister and Xagil. She shoved the money back at Lyons.

He shook his head. Lying to them, he showed them his travelers' checks. Then he grabbed the weapons, the clutter of discarded gifts—tape player, walkie-talkies, the shoes, the tangle of adhesive tape and socks—and shoved it all in his pack. With a quick *adios* he took his rifle and climbed up the slope. High uphill, he stopped. They had not pursued him. Peering through the trees, he looked for them. He waited a few minutes for the cloud mist to sweep past. Finally he caught a glimpse of the red *huipiles* Juana and Marylena wore. They had resumed their long climb down to the highway. When they reached the road they would join the other Quicheneros traveling to the city. They would be only three of many others, a teenage boy with two anonymous women and their children. With no *norteamericano* to betray them with his presence, they would pass through the surveillance and identity checks.

Obscuring their trail as he climbed—the trackers would know people had passed, but not how many—

Lyons returned to the ridge line where he had watched Nate die.

There he searched the mountainside until he found a deep crevice between two rocks. He took out Xagil's bandolier of Galil magazines and all the grenades. He unclipped a holstered 9mm pistol from a web belt. Then he dropped his bright-blue two-hundred-dollar pack—containing all his gear, the reclaimed gifts, the Uzi and the pistols—into the crevice. Kicking in dirt and leaves, he buried it, then sprinkled leaves on his tracks to the rocks.

Lyons found concealment and waited. Lying in dry brush, occasional flies finding him, he watched the ridge line for trackers. He viewed forest and clearings and jutting rocks. If a helicopter came, he had a view of the sky. If soldiers came, they had to pass his position. Time passed slowly.

The International wanted him. For interrogation. An interrogation conducted by doctors and specialists, with the assistance of drug injections, electroshock, torture. Lyons had no illusions. All men broke under drugs and torture. It took time, but the experts would have months, maybe years.

Years before, Mafia goons had questioned him for a week. A week of beatings and questions and days becoming nights becoming days again as he lapsed in and out of consciousness. But those goons had been amateurs, only sadists. The good time of beating and torturing a cop got in the way of the questions.

Only a week. The International would have doctors standing by in case of injury. They would monitor his heartbeat. They'd keep him alive until he became a talking vegetable. Betraying everyone. His friends, Stonyman, everyone who had ever helped Able Team.

Lyons knew how to avoid breaking under interrogation. A dead man didn't talk. Torture a corpse all you want, it won't talk. He had clipped the holstered 9mm autoloader to a bandolier. Checking it, he confirmed a round in the chamber. The pistol or a grenade would be his last defense, his ticket to peace.

A few days ago he had sprawled on the volcanic rocks overlooking Azatlan, a bottle of *aguardiente* in hand, and laughed at the idea of death. Now he didn't laugh. Silent, the Galil in his hands, he waited.

Rotor throb approached. Lyons checked his overhead cover and watched the sky. The noise varied, as if the helicopter crisscrossed the mountainsides. Then he saw it.

Camo-fatigued soldiers sat in the doors of the blue-and-white corporate aircraft, rifles in their hands. They looked down at the forest as the helicopter cruised at treetop level. Lyons saw the log on the tail boom, Trans-Americas SA.

The helicopter passed to the west. Lyons waited. Rotor throb returned, and the helicopter passed to the cast. The noise faded, then returned. Finally the helicopter continued to the west.

Following the trail north, Lyons reasoned. He continued waiting. He checked his watch. Only a few minutes after nine. Busy day. Nate died early. How much longer did he have?

He checked his map. Xagil and the women would have reached the road by now. With luck they would get a ride in a pickup truck to the highway. How much longer did he have to live?

Don't give up, dude! He said to himself, mimicking Gadgets's jive rhetoric. Work out a routine that'll give you a chance. Not that I think you got a chance....

If nothing happened on the ridge, he would cut down to the road and look for a squad waiting on the road. They wouldn't have walked when they could drive. Steal their truck, drive out of these mountains.

Another hour passed. Lyons spotted a hawk soaring in the cold wind. He watched the aerodynamics of the rust-colored bird of prey vary to meet the changing air currents, the tail flexing slightly, the angles of the wings shifting as the hawk looked first to one side, then another, soaring without effort as it hunted. Sunlight shimmered on the feathers.

Life, so marvelous and precious. Life, the sight of the sun on a bird in flight. Life, the dream.

The hawk spotted prey. Hovering, its wings moving in quick flutters, the hawk backpedaled in the sky, fixing its sights on its target. Life, hunting and killing.

The bird seemed to start, and, veering away to the north, the hawk disappeared. Lyons guessed why. He glanced around him, double-checking his moves agains the landscape.

Minutes later rotor throb returned. Lyons watched the sky, expecting to see the corporate helicopter. But this time a green Guatemalan army troopship appeared. Soldiers crowded the side doors. Hundreds of yards south the troopship descended to the ridge.

Through the pines he saw soldiers rush along the ridge. Seconds later the helicopter rose, the troop area empty. No one manned the door gun. The troopship had off-loaded no less than ten men. The troopship faded into the south.

Lyons waited. He saw soldiers moving through the trees and drifting mists. From time to time men checked the forest matting. Searching for tracks. Lyons straightened the cotter pins on two fragmentation grenades.

Two soldiers stopped at the edge of the ridge. They checked the ground where Lyons had watched the end of Nate's life. He knew they had spotted his footprints. He waited.

Rotors thundered overhead. He saw a flash of the blue-and-white helicopter. Lyons knew what had happened. The soldiers had found the tracks of the fugitives and called their commander. The commander would lead his men in the capture. Probably the same commander who had started all this, who had sent the first death squad, who had sent his soldiers into Azatlan, who had assigned the soldiers to ambush Nate and his family.

Who had taken away Nate's life. Who had left Marylena a widow with two small children.

"No matter what, you Fascist goon," Lyons uttered quietly, "you die. You don't get me alive, you don't go back, and Nate and me most definitely kick your ass in hell."

Soldiers moved from cover to cover in a loose skirmish line. A cloud swept past, but Lyons saw their shadowy forms. He saw two soldiers crouch together. One soldier pointed. The second man rushed in that direction. The soldier who had pointed motioned another soldier to join him. He sent that soldier to another area. Then he ran to a tree. He unfolded a map, glanced at it, shoved it back into a thigh pocket.

The commander. In addition to his Galil he wore a pistol. None of the other soldiers wore a pistol. Then the officer rushed through a patch of sunlight.

Lyons smiled at the sight of a red beret and mirrored sunglasses. That's my man.

Checking the setting of the rear sight aperture, Lyons pushed the fire-selector of his Galil down to full-auto. He peered through the hundred-yard peep sight. He brought the tip of the front post sight on line with the pine where the commander crouched. Lyons waited.

Rising from a crouch, the commander shifted his position. Lyons followed the movement, the commander's form filling the protective ring of the Galil's front sight. He put the blade on the commander's belt buckle and fired a long full-auto burst, seeing the commander lurch backward as a 5.56mm slug tore through him, the recoil of the first round lifting the rifle and shifting the aim, the other slugs impacting in his gut, his lungs, his heart, his brain, the last slugs screaming past his head as he flew back, already dead.

Lyons jerked the pins from two grenades, throwing one straight ahead and the other to the right. He searched the area for another target, saw a man prone. Lyons put a single shot through the soldier's forehead as the grenades banged, one-two, and the sprinted to the right—west, toward the foot trail.

Rifle fire tore past him as he wove and dodged through the pines, then dived into brush. The auto-fire continued. He grabbed a fist-size rock from the ground and heaved it down the slope. Then another. The rocks crashed through branches, tumbling, mak-

ing noise for twenty yards. The soldiers aimed at the
noise.

Waiting for the wind to drive a cloud past, Lyons
turned and crawled east. He stayed low in the mist,
gripping his Galil in both hands, sacrificing the skin
on his knees and elbows. He moved as fast as he
dared. Men ran through the forest, scything the brush
with autofire. Lyons kept his belly to the dirt, stopping every few seconds to listen for soldiers. The firing continued, but on the other side of the ridge the
mist seemed to change the sounds, to deaden or dis-
tort the voices and shooting. He continued crawling.
When the earth sloped down, he crawled faster, rocks
and debris tearing at him. But he didn't stand and run.
Jiving to himself, he cheered himself on with the voice
of his friend the Wizard.

Make like a snake, Ironman. You'll live longer.

25

As the soldiers rushed to the west, obeying his instructions and firing their rifles harmlessly into the trees, Gunther moved east. He knew his opponent. Carl Lyons would not try to outrun ten young men with automatic rifles. Not in unfamiliar mountains. Not when he could trick them and escape.

Gunther watched the brush. He stayed against a pine, standing in shadows and branches, only one eye exposed. With his fair skin and white-blond hair covered with green and black camouflage paste, he knew Lyons would not see him.

Fifty yards away, as mist cleared, a fern trembled. A branch shifted. Something moved there. Glaring sunlight bathed the scene. He saw the suggestion of a form in the grass and low brush. Gunther estimated Lyons's path and dropped. He cradled his custom-stocked and reworked Benelli semiautomatic shotgun in his elbows and crawled, keeping his camouflage-capped head down. He crawled twenty yards. He found a knob of rocks jutting out of the slope.

His body flowed over the smooth stone. The rocks gave Gunther a view downhill without raising his head.

Thirty yards away a leg and a boot went into a stand of weeds. The stalks shifted as a form crawled through the weeds, then the motion stopped. A forehead and eyes appeared, Lyons's eyes visible above the grass and matted leaves, the lower half of his face hidden.

Gunther did not move. He did not shift the shotgun. He did not try to aim. Only his eyes shifted, following Lyons as the desperate man crawled through an open patch to gain the concealment of another group of bushes.

But in front of those bushes, forty yards from Gunther, another patch of open area would expose Lyons again. Gunther eased backward half a body length, putting the 12-gauge shotgun to his shoulder, letting the front grip rest in his left hand. He sighted through the buckhorn rear sight, resting the front blade where Lyons would appear. With the middle of his straight trigger finger he touched the safety. He did not put his finger into the trigger guard. Gunther waited for his opponent to appear.

Far behind him, on the west side of the ridge, the firing died away. Lyons would move faster now. Gunther waited, watching over the sights of the shotgun.

Too much time passed.

Gunther reset the safety and crawled backward. Moving north, keeping his body in the forest matting of leaves and grasses, Gunther made crushing noises and snaps with every movement. He could not avoid it.

Crawling and sliding, exploiting the same drifting mists that concealed Lyons, Gunther shifted to the other side of the brush he had seen Lyons enter. Then he heard the sound of boots running, sliding. Gunther crouched, never standing to his full height. He went to one knee against a pine surrounded by saplings.

Through the latticework of crisscrossed branches, he saw Lyons dodging from tree to tree, moving fast, quickly leaving the ridge behind. Gunther watched him for a moment.

Lyons made a dash, stopped to check the slope behind him, then veered off in another direction. Moving, pausing, zigzagging, crouchwalking through shadows, disappearing in the gray drifting clouds, he left the soldiers far behind.

But not Gunther. As Lyons ran, crashing and sliding through the brush, Gunther dropped down the steep slope, never rising to his feet, using his boot soles to break a path, virtually sliding for a hundred yards. He ignored the rocks and sticks gouging his body.

Lyons appeared in snatches as Gunther slid and crouched and dropped. Then Lyons stopped and Gunther stopped. But Lyons had heard him. Gunther saw the American take cover behind a tree.

Neither man moved. Hundreds of yards above them the soldiers shouted to one another. A rifle fired. Motionless, Gunther saw the horizontal line of a rifle barrel against the forest as Lyons searched for a target.

He did not fire. Lyons would not betray his position without a positive target. Gunther watched the rifle barrel shift from one side of the tree to the other. A rock skipped down the mountainside. Gunther did not move. More rocks created noise and Gunther saw movement. He watched as Lyons dodged to another tree and stopped, surveying the mountainside over the sights of his rifle.

Lyons finally ran again.

Gunther waited, then continued his crouching, sliding drop. While Lyons zigzagged, making the most of the available cover, Gunther disregarded the threat of any other riflemen in the forest. He focused on Lyons. He assumed Lyons must be alone. His friend had died hours before. If any other riflemen ran with Lyons, Lyons would not have behaved like this. Gunther had seen him in action and knew how he acted.

If Gunther had made the wrong assumption, perhaps he would die. If not, he would get Lyons.

Gunther passed Lyons. Angling toward his opponent's line of descent, Gunther continued downhill.

Lyons stopped. Gunther went flat, stayed motionless. The angle of the mountain kept Gunther in a stooped position. He waited, watching. Dirt and leaves filled his shirt. Insects crawled over him. He watched for Lyons's next move.

There was silence for sixty seconds, then Gunther saw Lyons crouchwalking parallel to the slope, the pistol grip of the Galil rifle held in his left hand, his right hand grabbing brush and roots. Then Lyons lost his footing and slid down a few body lengths.

Gunther raised the shotgun and flicked off the safety. Lyons caught his fall and stopped, going into a crouch. Gunther did not move. A tangle of brush blocked their sight of one another. But Gunther, his face painted with splotches of green and black, his uniform camouflage patterned, had a distinct advantage over Lyons in his gray slacks and blue T-shirt. Though his black jacket helped his concealment, he stood out against the forest background.

Holding his shotgun at his shoulder, brush and weeds all around him, Gunther watched Lyons.

A wind-driven cloud grayed the scene, and Lyons whirled and ran in the opposite direction, angling downslope, hoping to escape in the mist. Gunther saw an open line of fire. He snap-sighted on the running man's back and squeezed the trigger.

The impact slammed Lyons forward. He tumbled down the slope, losing his rifle.

Sliding again, then running in quick crouching dashes, Gunther closed the distance, watching for a pistol to appear. Stunned, but still moving, Lyons scrambled through the brush, searching for his rifle. One arm flopped.

He saw Gunther approaching. Jerking a grenade from a bandolier under his jacket, he tried to pull the pin but his other hand did not rise to the pull-ring. He put the ring in his mouth to pull the pin.

Gunther shot him again, the hundred-gram neoprene slug slamming into his chest and throwing him back. The grenade flew away. Ignoring the chance of blast and shrapnel, Gunther continued forward, another round in the chamber, his finger on the trigger.

Lyons groaned, a long shuddering sound of rage and aggression. His one working hand reached for a pistol on the bandolier.

Firing one more time, the impact flinging the arm back, Gunther rushed Lyons and brought the butt of the shotgun down on the American's head, in a swift, brutal stroke.

He set the shotgun's safety and rolled Lyons over, securing the American's hands behind him with tempered-steel handcuffs. Then he threw several loops of cord around Lyons's ankles. A long length of cord went around his neck. Gunther passed the cord through the loops around his ankles and pulled it tight, forcing the semi-conscious man to arch backward, choking on the rope across his throat. Lyons could not move without strangling.

Gunther checked Lyons's pulse. Strong.

Only then did Gunther accept victory.

He had taken Carl Lyons alive.

MORE GREAT ACTION COMING SOON

ABLE TEAM

#20 Shot to Hell

Honduran Hellground

An American journalist is tortured and murdered in Central America, but not before he tips off a CIA operative to the presence of Russian XCT missiles in the Honduran jungle. The Pentagon looks for a small mobile team to go in and neutralize the threat and comes up with the three strike-force veterans of Able Team. But somebody deep in the American war office is out to make sure Able Team's mission is a one-way ticket to hell.

Enter the
'Gear Up For Adventure Sweepstakes'
You May Win a 1986 AMC Jeep® CJ
Off-road adventure — Only in a Jeep®.

OFFICIAL RULES
No Purchase Necessary

1) To enter print your name, address and zip code on an Official Entry or on a 3" x 5" piece of paper. Enter as often as you choose but only one entry allowed to each envelope. Entries must be postmarked by January 17, 1986 and received by January 31, 1986. Mail entries first class. In Canada to Gold Eagle Gear Up For Adventure Sweepstakes, Suite 233, 238 Davenport Rd., Toronto, Ontario M5R 1J6. In the United States to Gold Eagle® Gear Up For Adventure Sweepstakes, P.O. Box 797, Cooper Station, New York, New York 10276. Sponsor is not responsible for lost, late, misdirected or illegibile entries or mail. Sweepstakes open to residents 18 years or older at entry of Canada (except Quebec) and the United States. Employees and their immediate families and household of Harlequin Enterprises Limited, their affiliated companies, retailers, distributors, printers, agencies, American Motors Corporation and RONALD SMILEY INC. are excluded. This offer appears in Gold Eagle publications during the sweepstakes program and at participating retailers. All Federal, Provincial, State and local laws apply. Void in Quebec and where prohibited or restricted by law.

2) First Prize awarded is a 1986 Jeep CJ with black soft top and standard equipment. Color and delivery date subject to availability. Vehicle license, driver license, insurance, title fees and taxes are the winner's responsibility. The approximate retail value is $8,500 U.S./$10,625 Canadian. 10 Second Prizes awarded of a Sports Binocular. The approximate retail value is $90 U.S./$112.50 Canadian. 100 Third Prizes awarded of Gold Eagle Sunglasses. The approximate retail value is $6.95 U.S./$8.65 Canadian. No substitution, duplication or cash redemption of prizes. First Prize distributed from U.S.A.

3) Winners will be selected in random drawings from all valid entries under the supervision of RONALD SMILEY INC. an independent judging organization whose decisions are final. Odds of winning depend on total number of entries received. First prize winner will be notified by certified mail and must return an Affidavit of Compliance within 10 days of notification. Winner residents of Canada must correctly answer a time-related arithmetical skill-testing question. Affidavits and prizes that are refused or undeliverable will result in alternate winners randomly drawn. The First Prize winner may be asked for the use of their name and photo without additional compensation. Income tax and other taxes are prize winners' responsibility.

4) For a major prize winner list, Canadian residents send a stamped, self addressed envelope to Gold Eagle Winner Headquarters, Suite 157, 238 Davenport Road, Toronto, Ontario M5R 1J6. United States residents send a stamped, self-addressed envelope to Gold Eagle Winner Headquarters, P.O. Box 182, Bowling Green Station, New York, NY 10274. Winner list requests may not include entries and must be received by January 31, 1986 for response.

A division of
WORLDWIDE LIBRARY®

GOLD EAGLE

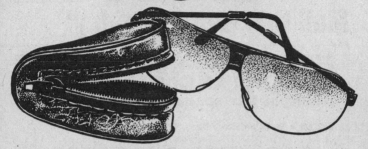

GET THE NEW WAR BOOK AND MACK BOLAN BUMPER STICKER FREE!

Mail this coupon today!